SHELLEY AVENUE

A novel by Robby Sheils

Shelley Avenue — By: Robby Sheils

Copyright © 2021 Robby Sheils

Golden Smelt Publishing

All rights reserved. No portion of this book may be reproduced in any form without permission from the publisher, except as permitted by U.S copyright law. For permissions contact: goldensmeltpublishing@gmail.com

978-0-578-33886-6

First Edition

For Mom, Dad, Tommy, and Paddy

TOC

"Now and then,
in this workaday world,
things do happen in the delightful story-book fashion,
and what a comfort that is."

\-   **Louisa May Alcott**

PROLOGUE

THE finale of a show that starred miracles and tragedies took form in a warm and rosy circle, laying itself down and letting go (as it always does). The millions and millions of movements that reverberated all over the state would slow down now to make soft waves—rocking, rocking, rocking. Before the day had ended, a newly divorced woman living somewhere off in the country let her screen door open so her dog could get some air and do its business. Down the road from the divorcee and the dog, a mailman was finishing up the last loop of his daily commute. Even further down the road from the mailman, a baseball game between two towns was going ten innings deep. The year was 1975—no, 1995? It was something. Anglers sped up and down a labyrinth of roads in their G1s and Broncos in high hopes of catching the flies at twilight. Leaves were falling across the Greenville hills, and many miles to the east and far down the coast, tulips were popping up in Portland cul-de-sacs. An old man sat under a beat awning and wrote in his journal: *Early Wake Up Before the Spring Day with the Hail, '84.* One of the baseball teams from the game down the road from the mailman eventually won on a walk-off passed ball (took eleven innings!). A group of neighborhood friends were starting their long climb down from the high limbs in a white pine; one of them brought a big box of donuts that they planned on sharing once they touched down. The scenes being illustrated have no apparent relationship to the soon-to-be-mentioned boy himself; rather, they create an outline of sorts. The game, the tree, the mail, the dog, the poop; even the donuts—no, *especially* the donuts. All of them help construct the story in which we find the boy operating within. I guess that's gonna become pretty obvious. Still worth a mention.

THREDSUM, MAINE

2001

I

IT was the coldest night of the new year. A massive red house sat in front of over fifty acres of blueberry bushes, all of which were awaiting their annual summer resurrection. Neighboring the bushes was even more land, stretching all four directions until they hit defined lines of darkness. The surrounding fields made the home look smaller than it actually was, and its glowing yellow lights and puffing chimney made it seem like a beating heart was within its center. On unforgivingly cold winter nights, the lamps and smoke gave the impression that it was warmer than all other homes, and all the more welcoming at that. Within its brick walls, an argument between siblings was taking place.

"Well, that's that," said the eldest sister with an air of satisfaction.

"No, you switched them!" argued her younger brother.

"*No*, I didn't!"

As the victor of drawing the shortest straw, thirteen-year-old Noah Libby had been picked from his siblings to journey to the attic and return a forgotten ornament. The family's Christmas tree had been out on the sidewalk for four days before the mother of four had put her foot down—someone was going to make the trip whether they liked it or not. No one wanted to; the attic smelled so heavily of mildew that it clung to any clothes that got near it. There were dust mites everywhere, too; it was a suicide mission for anyone with allergies—a hypersensitivity the siblings shared.

Reluctant to carry out his task, Noah stalled a whole day until his parents had threatened to not give him any supper. Eventually, he climbed the stairs, and then again, walked down a long hall, pulled a chair out from his bedroom and into the hallway, stood on it, reached to the ceiling, flipped a latch, and watched a ladder swing down from above and nearly hit his head. Merry songs that were being sung by his two younger siblings came echoing up the stairs—this time a tone-deaf rendition of "Chestnuts Roasting on An Open Fire" that would make The Great King roll in his grave. The palpable magic of Christmastime had been gradually wearing off since the new year had arrived, yet carols and cookies from those who sang kept wonders floating throughout the house.

Noah climbed up the steps of splintered cedar, eventually reaching a small and stuffy room with dramatically sloped ceilings. Upon reaching the platform, he tied a t-shirt around his face, fastening it with a slip knot like he would a bandana. It didn't help much, as he still felt dust tickle his throat and could smell mold all around. Bent over, he squinted at boxes and cabinets in search of where he should put the small ceramic Santa he held in his right hand. The only light in the room came from the lamps in the corridor below and a faint orange sunset ahead. Never spending more than fifteen or so seconds where he was now, Noah had forgotten about the tiny porthole window in the attic. He contemplated getting a flashlight from the basement. Being at the highest point in his house, he instead decided to get by with squinting and adjusting to the darkness. Curious about the view from the forgotten window, he made his way over to the far end of the wooden planks and looked out onto the vast farmland his family owned.

The perspective was stunning. Noah felt as though he was an osprey perched on its nest, peeking over the yard he once considered to be a master of. Directly beneath him, he could see the clogs of leaves in the gutters that his father always complained about, and to his left, if he pressed the right side of his face all the way next to the glass, he could see an unusually large bald patch on the top of a tree; it was a gigantic elm that the Libby's had collectively agreed must be older than any other tree on their farm. Noah had remembered the times he'd linked hands with his siblings to try and wrap their arms around the entire circumference of it. Still, he'd never noticed the missing branches he could now spot. The view straight ahead was remarkable, too. The boy could look out on the land for miles and miles; the sloping hills curtained themselves like waves ebb towards the sunset. He had to pull up his sleeve constantly to wipe the window clear of the fog from his breath.

When the sun had retired and the woods on the horizon had turned into a deep shade of blue, Noah decided it was time to make his way downstairs. The room had become extremely dark after the sun had set, and so he bent over again and walked gingerly in the direction of the hallway light. He tapped several cardboard boxes with his feet on his way over to the opening in the floor—his ears raised to listen. After he heard the shimmering ring of sleigh bells, Noah gently placed the Santa in his home for the next eleven months.

Just before he was to step down on the highest rung of the ladder, though, he accidentally kicked another box. The sound it made was almost identical to the one he'd just tapped. At first thought, Noah worried that he might have placed the ornament in the wrong package. He picked up the box and tilted it towards the faint yellow light, all the while hypothesizing what could've emulated the faint and ineffable sound of sleigh bells.

It felt much lighter than the first one, and, unsurprisingly, harbored few items. Inside, an ancient set of sleigh bells sat at the top. It looked like they were the only holiday-themed item in there, though. Accompanying the bells was a delicate-looking watch, along with a binder, a few silver rings, some loose paperwork, a moss green book with an evergreen on its cover, and what appeared to be a postcard with a yellow postage stamp in its corner.

Writing was scribbled down on the card, but between the dark lighting and the slashed penmanship, Noah couldn't read a word of it. As he couldn't make anything out, he never discovered that the card was written by his grandmother. A single mother of two and an uncertified chess master, Mackenzie Fanning had resided in Maine from her birth in Rangeley to her death in Bridgton. None of her grandchildren had ever met her, and thus knew nothing about her identity and personality, yet there Noah stood—unknowingly inches away from discovering her voice. The words on the postcard were written a long time ago. In fact, they were the last ones she'd sent to her daughter.

As Mackenzie's letter awaited Noah to read its body, the home below noisily moved about. Stairs creaked, voices murmured, doors were pulled open and slammed closed. From room to room, feet pounded on faded wooden floorboards and hands brushed over old white walls. Beneath, besides, and above them, though, were pairs of patient eyes and ears, constantly existing as spectators to all acts of good and evil. As forbearing as they were, the onlookers always waited until the moon would rise high and the house would fall silent to move about its halls; it was then that the house was truly theirs to roam unnoticed.

The warm smells of challah bread and tomato soup had crept its way through the home and up the rungs to where the boy stood. His stomach made an audible grumble, and instinctively he put down the card and ran towards the kitchen. And so, the lines kept collecting dust on the back of a photo worn by time, stuck in an attic sparsely visited throughout the year, perfectly immobile in the loneliest corner of a gigantic farmhouse.

II

THE six bowls of soup had been finished in a matter of minutes after the youngest of the Libby's, Samuel, had finished saying his prayers. The closing words contained a small mention on how he was grateful for the warm dinner, but mostly concentrated on a wish for winter break to continue with a snow day tomorrow.

As his family traveled through the best and worst parts of their Sunday, Noah daydreamed about missing his test on *The Fundamental American Authors of the 20th Century* tomorrow morning. The temperature outside was certainly making Samuel's prayer a possibility. Every hour of the day had been below zero degrees Fahrenheit, with winds that made Western Maine feel like Northern Alaska. The Libby's lived in Thredsum, a hilly town in Somerset County with a population of three thousand and seventy-five. The tiny town held only a dozen storefronts, as most businesses in the county were based out of the neighboring seat of Skowhegan. Between the twelve was a bookstore, a Wendy's, and a blacksmith. Almost all the others were little country stores that sold all things from car tires to bacon-egg-and-cheese sandwiches. Being inland meant that summers in Thredsum were hot. However, that isn't to say that the weather stayed consistent year-round. On the night Noah had returned the ornament, the air was so frigid that by nighttime it crept its way into the dining and living rooms, coaxing everyone at the table to put on sweaters or puffed coats.

Noah had devoted his entire Sunday to lie around indoors and listen to Samuel shout down the halls with updates on the cold front. Luckily for both boys, neither had to be outside to experience what Samuel had described. The same couldn't be said about their father.

Patrick Libby was a large man with a curly beard that fit his impressive stature. While everyone else was still working on their first bowls, he had gotten seconds, and then thirds. His cheeks were rosy from the wind and his lips chapped from the cold. He'd spent the entirety of his day outside, cutting down trees for firewood and marking the spots where he'd set traps to catch any animals that dared steal from *Libby's Locally Owned Blueberry Field*. Come springtime, he'd go back out and set the traps up. Now was the time to eat and wait. With his last taste of tomato-soaked bread, Mr. Libby leaned back into his chair so deep that the front legs lifted off from the dining room floor.

"Thank you, Clare," he murmured with half opened eyes to his wife across the table. The tall blonde woman that sat opposite him smiled back and replied confidently that he was welcome. After responding, she looked Samuel's way and gave him a wink.

Noah's mother was the most symmetrical person he'd ever seen. Her nose pointed to the ground like an arrow, and her great blue eyes could pierce anyone else's that looked her way. She was almost as tall as her husband, nearing six feet. Claire Libby was the mastermind behind the farm, even though she was a gifted baker by nature; her mother had spent most of her years kneading dough on dry wood and flour in a tiny bakery beneath her home. Managing the farm had scratched out any plans to pursue the ancestral practice professionally, and, in addition to her workload, she never cared for 'perpetuating the stereotype of maternal culinary devotion' (as she so eloquently put it). She loved baking, and she loved cooking, and she hated her husband's attempts. Thus, it was a tough battle for her to win. She spent slow weeknights and weekend mornings cooking shortbreads, sourdoughs, pies, crisps, cakes, an assortment of cookies, brownies, blondies, crepes, galettes, along with other experiments that would comprise a list of comical length. She loved hugs and wouldn't go to bed until each of her children got one from her. Almost every day she dressed herself in a sweater, and this evening was no exception. In the past, Noah's friends had told him they were intimidated by his mother, which thoroughly confused him. Maybe it was her height. To him, his mother was the warmest person in the entire world.

Noah hadn't inherited his mother's impressive height, at least not yet. That gene had been passed down to his only older sibling, Mackenzie. If his mother was the most symmetrical person he'd ever seen, his sixteen-year-old sister was a close runner-up. Her hair was brown in contrast to her mother's blonde, yet it flowed in a similarly enchanting way. She had the palest skin in the family and freckles that dotted her nose and cheeks. Accompanying her pretty face were pointed ears that she constantly hid behind her long brunette waves. Being the oldest of all the siblings, she'd been named after their mother's mother. In recent months, she'd asked her family to refer to her by her full name, rather than 'Mack'. However, to her dismay, no one had adjusted to the switch.

"Sit up," she said, glaring down at her younger brother.

With a groan, Noah pushed his body up so his head no longer leaned on the back of the chair. Mack's quiet order had been the only words she'd spoken to him the whole day. Noah couldn't imagine she viewed him as being a friend. While she *was* unduly standoffishness towards her little brother, Mack had little to no problem discussing her accomplishments with her parents.

"Could you believe she gave me *that* as an extra credit question?" asked Mack; she had her eyebrows raised and her head tilted towards the end of the table. Mack's father gave a lazy nod in her general direction; he still had his eyes closed and was struggling not to doze off. Noah would mostly see his older sister in the kitchen eating snacks, or sometimes in the living room reading. Otherwise, she was down the road at one of her friends' places or in her bedroom studying something or other. Although she was only three years older than him, Noah felt a divide between him and his sister. She'd already begun talking to her parents about colleges, and whenever Noah would ask her a question, she almost always answered with: "I'll tell you when you're older."

Noah felt much closer to his younger sister, Sharon. The ten-year-old sat across the table from him, crisscross applesauce, reciting every county in Maine (via song) to their mother in her hoarse voice. She had long blonde hair, all the way down to her hip—looped in a pony and dyed purple on the ends. Her parents always referred to her as a 'firecracker', and Samuel called her Sharpoo. Despite her reputation as a bull in a china shop, Sharon had great control over her own feelings. In fact, she was as emotionally self-sufficient as fifth graders come. As Noah saw it, she never relied on anyone else for happiness. To the left of Sharon, Samuel was whining to their father.

"But Maddy likes it," argued Samuel.

"Maddy may like it—Maddy may even love it," his father replied tiredly, "but Maddy's stomach *hates* it."

"But look at her!"

Underneath their long oak dinner table and next to Samuel's swinging legs, the Libby's lazy chocolate lab was going to town on a bowl of leftover tomato soup and sour cream. Noah's father took a deep breath in and turned his attention to his other son.

"Did you go up yet?"

Noah nodded; the ornament was back in the box with the rest of them.

III

DINNER had ended. Plates were cleared from the table and were soon to be washed in the sink. Noah's mother had put out snickerdoodle cookies she'd made the night before as dessert, and his father was preparing a fire in the living room. Sharon and Samuel had run off as soon as their bowls had touched the sink, and Mack and Noah had both stayed to help their mother clean the pots and pans. Noah normally dreaded helping in the kitchen and stalled until he was called to do so, but tonight was different. On wintry nights, like the one that was now upon him, the third floor of his house was always susceptible to cold air finding its way through cracks Noah couldn't find. The kitchen, now lit up and sweating from the open oven, was the warmest spot in the house. As for his room, two duvets were nicely laid across his sinking bed, stuffed liberally with feathers of all sorts and plumped by his mother to reach a height and width that resembled a rolling landscape of marshmallows. Noah loved the nights when he felt as if he needed a jacket to walk the halls—the untucking and hopping into a fully made bed was worth all the shivers he'd shake off to get there. He just needed to warm up a bit before making the journey.

Despite not moving around much all day, he felt exhausted, and just like he'd done earlier at the table, Noah drifted off into his thoughts; the sounds of pans clashing and soap bubbles popping served as a backdrop to ideas that would drift by. The sound of his name being called brought him back to the reality he'd temporarily abandoned.

"—and I know she's hard on you," said Noah's mother, now with her sweater rolled to where her cuffs barely reached her elbows, looking down at her hands scrubbing away the insides of a tomato-stained pot. Her eyes darted in Noah's direction twice to signal her anticipation of a response.

"Who?"

"Mackenzie."

At the sound of her name, Noah looked to his right. He fully expected to see his older sister drying utensils with a towel and organizing mason jars and glass cups in the cupboards. Instead, the utensils had disappeared, the glasses already lined up back in their homes. Mack was nowhere to be seen. The whole scene was confusing to Noah; his mother could've been done with her dishes by now, too—she hated doing dishes. Usually, she'd do a quick wipe and call it a good day.

"What?" he asked.

Noah's mother stopped scrubbing in circles for a fraction of a second. "Were you even listening to me?"

"You said Mack is hard on me."

She raised her eyebrows.

"And—" continued Noah, "—and I agree."

Instead of carrying to respond, she laughed and lightly shook her head. Noah didn't know what to say.

"Nice try, but no—that's not what I wanted you to get out of this." In between her words she'd stopped scrubbing, turned the sink on, washed her hands, and then the pot, before going to work on the spoons that'd been busy bathing in soapy water. "Your sister *is* hard on you, but you can't take that personally," she said, her voice now lowered into a whisper. "She has a lot of things going on nowadays, you know. Just last month we started looking at colleges for her, and you know how she is about that stuff."

Noah's mother gave him a prolonged look that made him shift in his shoes; he *didn't* know how she was about that stuff. He never paid any attention to it. She eventually stopped staring at him and turned back to her spoons.

"Well, she tries very, very, very hard in school for her future. She wants to get into a good college more than anything—it's what drives her to do all the work that she does."

Noah followed what his mother said, but he couldn't get behind any of what she was telling him.

"She doesn't have to be a jerk to me just because she tries hard in school," said Noah.

"Noah," said his mother with a sigh, "acting like that is all part of growing up."

"Then I don't wanna do that."

"What?"

"I don't wanna grow up."

She laughed again—softer than before.

"I know, but we all have to do it at some point or another."

Noah couldn't respond; the words he wanted to say out loud stuck in his throat like peanut butter. He felt as though the conversation didn't apply to him. In his mind, he didn't have to grow up, and he never had to become like Mack.

In the living room, near the fireplace that now blazed with waves of bright orange heat, a heavily scarred hand beckoned Noah to come over. His father was stretched out on the far seat of the long couch that filled the room, his legs crossed at the ankle on a coffee table, his back sunk into the cushion, his hands locked into each other and acting as a net for his tipped head. It would take a whole crowd of men to get him to stand up from where he sat.

"You know the markers, right?"

Noah knew what the markers were; they were placed on the perimeter of the field to mark the spots where traps were going to be set. He nodded.

"Okay, good. Well, I may've left a pile of them out by the rock. Came around the far side and was too hungry to go back. It's not too far."

Noah understood his father was waiting for him to agree to collect the pile of markers he'd forgotten about, but because of his reluctance to do so, Noah chose to focus his attention towards the chessboard on the coffee table instead. The pieces were arranged on the blocks in such a way that told the story of dinner being ready; it was a game abandoned, yet to be resumed. While Noah stalled, Sharon had run into the room to snatch her new drawing journal that she'd left on the coffee table.

"Would you get them for me?"

Noah nodded while keeping his eyes on the chessboard. He was well aware that his father could easily wait until a warm and sunny morning and get the markers himself, but that wasn't how he liked to do things. Ever since Noah started sixth grade, his old man had been asking him to do all sorts of odd jobs around the farm at less-than-ideal times; it was all done in the hopes of turning his first son into 'a true Mainer', though Noah didn't understand what he meant by that. His father's legs were still crossed in the notch between his right shin and foot, his head still leaned back lazily into his palms. If it would take a whole crowd to move him, there was no hope in a thirteen-year-old arguing.

* * *

Samuel's constant updates on the weather outside couldn't prepare Noah for the wickedness of the air that hit his face upon opening and exiting his mudroom door. Even with four layers covering his chest, he could still feel his core begin to freeze. In his right hand, on top of a thick red mitten, was a faded yellow flashlight; it was the only item that Noah had brought with him on his mission. The landscape was dark, and not a star could be seen in the sky above him. A covering of clouds had silently rolled across the night's sky while Noah's family had played *rose, bud, thorn,* and ate bubbling soup. Despite the clouds that blocked the stars, Noah knew exactly where he was walking towards. In the daytime, the wide and flat boulder known as 'the rock' would stick out like a sore thumb from the flat acres of farmland and dark backdrop of the woods. Despite its unassuming name, it was Noah's headquarters—the main spot he'd camp out of during countless hours of playing outside. In the wintertime it was the largest snowball fort in the land, and in autumn it was a mountain he'd climb and conquer. In the summer, he often would lay down on its sloped back and watch the clouds swirl into each other and pass by with a girl he had a crush on. Her name was Maegan.

Across the fields came a carpet of sound. Waves of warm deep chord progressions cut through the frost and streams of wind; it was the music of a deep cello, and it flooded out from the only other home in the surrounding land besides Noah's own. Some ways north and on the other side of Shelley Avenue (the main road that ran next to the Libby house), six golden squares lit up the night sky. They lined up perfectly with one another like a half-dozen sheet pan of muffins. The outside of the house was ghost white, and its door and windows a deep blue. It was an enormous home that only belonged to a father and his son—the Bonson's. The Bonson boy's name was Frederick; he was older than Mack, and in June he'd finish high school for good. The music he played had never not been lovely. Tonight, as it stretched across the fields and into the edge of the woods, though, it sounded lonelier than it ever had before. He rarely had seen Fredrick outside of his home; he was like a painting to Noah, framed in navy shutters and playing songs for no one.

Noah was only a few feet in front of the rock when he could make out a clump of wires that leaned against it. After he'd reached down and picked up the lot, he stopped to stare at the clouds. They'd all stopped moving. Because he'd waddled outside in a suit that was composed of cotton and polyester, Noah hadn't been able to hear over his swishing just how silent everything around him was until now. He normally wasn't afraid of the dark, but the chills that snuck down his spine made him think twice. It took a minute to study the landscape before paranoia bested him. He pointed his flashlight across the edge of the woods, only being able to penetrate a foot into the miles and miles of trees that were in front of him.

Back in June of the previous year, during a campfire his counselor had prepared for him and his bunkmates, Noah remembered how everyone partook in a discussion on whether they'd rather spend a night sleeping alone in the middle of the field or in the middle of the woods. The overnight camp in this memory was an all-boys establishment in Eastern Maine, hundreds of miles away from Thredsum and on a lake near the sea. The conversation happened only a few nights before the end of his three-week session in late August. The sky had looked distinctly different from how it did now; back then, there'd been tens of thousands of stars sparkling above him and his friends. On nights like those, Noah's counselors let the cabin stay up later than normal. After curfew had come and gone, all the boys would trade stories about their lives back home. No one else in the entire camp was from Thredsum. Along with sports, it was common for girls to be in constant conversation. Inside the cabin, some boys even hid pictures of love interests from back home underneath their beds. They were stuffed in cardboard shoe boxes, layered underneath long letters from friends and unread books only brought to please mothers. He remembered the stories that came along with the pictures, too. First kisses, movie dates, random gossip, unverified bragging; they were all commonplace. He also remembered that he'd answered with woods.

That, however, was when he was surrounded by his friends, a fire, and was just a stone's throw away from where he'd soon be sleeping. Now that he stood here, though, at the partition between vast and dense, he understood the horror of the woods. He hadn't the slightest of ideas of what could be beyond the trunks and leafless branches. Upon staring into the dark, he realized that animals, no matter how grizzly they'd be, weren't what frightened him. What really got to him that night, and what made the hairs on his neck prick up, was the thought of someone watching him. A pair of eyes could be looking at a boy standing alone next to a big rock in a wide-open field and the boy would have no clue. A set of supernatural eyes, like binoculars, and a face with no nose and no mouth; they belonged to an apparition—staring, listening, and waiting. Noah felt it in his bones, moving in his marrow. A ghost was out there, creeping noiselessly and waiting for the right moment to come out and take him. He was sure of it.

Noah quickly readjusted the wires in his arms and walked back in the mudroom's direction. As unrealistic imaginations danced themselves into the front of his mind, he couldn't help but monitor the trees to his right. Despite momentary glances towards the path back to his home, he stayed scanning the perimeter of the forest. Shadows and poor lighting gave the illusion of fingers resting on trees, or legs lying horizontally on the ground. Whenever cars passed by on Shelley Avenue he heard whispers, and whenever he whipped his flashlight back and forth, he couldn't help but imagine faces—ones that were as horrifying as he could conjure.

He'd nearly made his way back to the front lawn before he heard a clunk beneath his chest. A few wires had tipped out of his hands and fallen on the dead grass. As he regathered the pieces, he felt his knees and elbows chafe. Noah kept the light shining in the trees. Everything about the woods was as still and uniform as possible. However, one spot caught his eye. The shine from his light revealed a pocket with an odd array of colors; along with green, brown, gray, and black, there was crimson. Although slight, the light bounced off the red in a way that sparkled strangely. His feet were already walking towards the sight before his mind had made up whether or not he dared to move any closer. As Noah crossed the edge of the forest, the red grew, the light now mirroring off the glazed surface so strongly it blinded him. He took two steps closer before he stopped in his tracks and the surface revealed itself before him.

Down on its side, surrounded by flies, ticks, mosquitos, and grubs, was the carcass of a dead deer. From what Noah could gather, it was young. A mighty thick and sharp stick from a collapsed tree trunk had pierced its neck. The belly of it'd been stripped. No fur was left. The muscle and tissue were taut and almost completely unmarked. A deep red approaching a shade of black blanketed the ground. Its eyes were still open, and it almost looked as if it was staring back at Noah's flashlight. Disturbing as it was, the image reminded him of something quite the contrary. For some odd reason, the bare body of the deer instantly resurrected a memory of him and his family in Belfast, a small town almost halfway up the coast of his home state; they'd been up there for a race Mack had back when she was in middle school and used to run track. After a massive celebratory post-race lunch (she got second!), the Libby crew had stepped out onto the chipped bricks with full bellies and a collective desire for sweets. As tiny as the downtown of Belfast is, it didn't take long at all to find a spot and settle their cravings. The candy shop, of what Noah could remember, was as small as any store he'd ever stepped into. The walls had been stocked to the ceiling with tens of glass boxes, all filled to their brims with categorized candies, from sours to chocolates and from licorices to gums. Next to the window, a taffy machine spun its arms round and round as an exhibit for those who walked past it on the sidewalk. Not only was the red of the stretched candy the same shade as the breast of the deer, but its texture was incredibly similar as well—it must've been, at least; otherwise, why would he have recalled such an obscure memory?

Noah stared at the spot until his eyes had to turn away and his shoulders shivered. He stood up, spun his flashlight around, and walked his way back to the mudroom. Goosebumps kept popping up in fear he was being followed. He began his walk at a brisk pace, but soon switched to a jog. It didn't take long for him to sprint.

Inside now, Noah threw his boots off, stripped his layers, and raced into the kitchen. Upon looking into the living room, he saw that the fire his father had prepared earlier had died down significantly, which forced Maddy to inch herself closer to the source. She'd moved so close to the fire that her ears were now nearly touching the ash. Meanwhile, the family's white and ginger-spotted cat, Percy, crouched on the base of the only windowsill in the room. Percy almost always spent his days and nights manning the barn, but it seemed the cold weather had forced him to migrate into the main house. His eyes were pointed to the floor, flitting up and down and from left to right, searching for mice that would never come.

Noah's mother was also in the living room, reading a book and lying down on their wide maroon rug, with her back against the short side of their long L shaped couch. His father was in the same spot that he'd sat down in after dinner, wrapped up in blankets and cozy. The chess board and its pieces hadn't moved the slightest bit. Everyone else, it seemed, had gone up to their rooms. The embers behind his mother fluttered weakly, a lame attempt at begging for another log to be put on. Noah wondered how lengthy his trip outside was. Despite the weak fire, the room was still toasty, causing the lone window in the room to fog up. Outside, the snow Samuel had prayed for quietly began to fall.

IV

THE morning after he'd seen the deer, Noah was woken up from a dim glow that gleamed through his window and onto several half-read books still spread open on his bedroom floor. Seeing as it was already light out, he inferred that his school bus wasn't coming to get him and that he'd be enjoying his first snow day of the new year. A rush of relief surged through his frame as he propped himself up on his bed and adjusted his position, sitting up straight and stretching out his head to be able to get a better view of the world outside his window.

The sky was still cloudy, and the last flakes were drifting towards the half foot layer of snow beneath them. Because so few were falling, Noah could focus on individual crystals as they fluttered their way past his window; they swayed side to side, and sometimes even defied gravity in an upwind. It looked as if each flake was competing to be the last one to touch the ground. Heaves of snow were capped on the fanning branches of evergreens that lined the fields. They looked fake, like sugar cookies with green sprinkles and mounds of icing. He couldn't help but smile.

Somehow, he'd found an avenue through the clothes and books that covered his floor and made his way to a badly maintained bureau. Drawers had sleeves and pant legs falling out of them, along with nails which stuck out from where knobs should be. Above the dresser hung a wide mirror with a silver Victorian frame; its borders looked like the stalks of a shimmering grape vine that slowly twisted itself around perfect right angles, framing the reflection of a scrawny and well-slept teenage boy with bedhead.

Noah had blonde hair like his mother's, but as years had gone on it'd turned brown like Mack's. He had a straight nose, but the eyes that neighbored it were quite crooked, and were especially asymmetrical when he looked at his own reflection. He lacked freckles, and in the winter months he constantly had chapped lips. His body was, and always had been, particularly smaller and skinnier than most of his friends, despite hearing from relatives each year that a growth spurt would be right around the corner. Following a hard ruffle from his hand on the top of his head, Noah prepared an outfit in which he'd laze around in all day. After settling on red plaid sweatpants and a bright purple *Libby's Locally Owned Blueberry Field* t-shirt, he set off across the house in anticipation of finding pancakes and bacon.

No two rooms in the main house were farther apart than the kitchen and Noah's bedroom. If one looked at the farm from the street, they'd see that the main house was separated into three bright red blocks, descending like big scarlet Russian nesting dolls. On the far right was the smallest of the three segments; it had a flat roof on top of its single story and was hugged by a beautiful wrap-around porch, enveloping its sturdy brick walls with white wicker. Beneath the section's horizontal roofing were a mudroom, a tiny bathroom, and a kitchen.

To its left stood a two-story home that appeared to be decades old, but not because it appeared to be poorly furnished—no, not at all. In fact, the middle section of the house was the most well kept out of the three. Rather, it was the six symmetrical street facing windows and two porch lanterns that made it look recognizably colonial. Behind the flat face and inside its walls were four bedrooms, a bathroom, a living room, an office, a playroom (which also was the first aid station of the house), and the dining room. One of the bedrooms was his parents'—the biggest of them all, which had a bed longer and wider than all the rest in the house. Noah was the only member of his family that didn't live in the middle house. Instead, his room was in the last and tallest block all the way to the left.

Rather than staying consistent with the brickwork of the other two segments, the outside of the tallest section was covered in wood paneling. The panels were painted red to match the middle home, but it clearly hadn't worked; the shade that Noah's father had picked was something more of a salmon, clashing horribly with the rest of the main house. Inside Noah's section, atop a long, narrow, and creaky staircase, was his room, a bathroom, a hallway, and the attic he'd visited. Below it all was a great open space that stored a tractor and a broken harvester, along with hundreds and hundreds of crates.

Before Patrick and Clare Libby had celebrated the purchase of their first home over a steak dinner, the farmhouse had belonged to another family. In fact, it belonged to another one before that, and even another one before *that.* In its past, all the farmhouse's walls had been white, and come wintertime were covered by huge rugs as insulation. The physical remains of the original home were few and far between. Sometimes Noah's father would announce that he'd 'found a nail from another lifetime!', but that was about it. The atmosphere of the home, though, was something that existed on a supernatural and transcendental level—a presence which encapsulated the rough and handsome soul of Maine; it was constant and timeless.

Full of excitement and thanks, Noah skipped down the stairs and through the subsiding levels of his home. He hadn't yet caught wafts of fresh bacon but could've sworn he heard the sizzle of batter bubbling on the griddle. To his dismay, he was also beginning to hear what sounded like teenage girls arguing. It seemed that his ears hadn't deceived him; for Mack had two of her friends over in their kitchen, and both looked thoroughly upset. Noah's entrance had gone unnoticed.

"You're a liar!"

"I knew you had them; I knew it!"

Both girls kept berating Mack until she conceded into giving them a response.

"It's not a big deal!" she shot back while waving a spatula high in the air. Noah still hadn't a clue what they were bickering about.

"Seriously, Mackenzie," began the shorter of the two girls, "you *live* on a blueberry farm. Don't you eat enough of them?"

Not answering her question, Mack walked over to the griddle and flipped six blueberry pancakes over on themselves. Noah walked his way over to the far side of the kitchen, avoiding any eye contact, and went to pour himself a glass of water. When he'd reached the cabinet, he could see outside onto his side yard, now covered in a blanket of white. Trudging his way (somewhat uncoordinatedly) out deeper and deeper into the fields of snow was Samuel, who looked to be thoroughly enjoying what had happened overnight.

"Noah, what would you rather have in your pancakes?" asked the taller of the two guests. The girl interrogating Noah happened to be a family friend in which he'd known for most of his life; her name was Shauna. She was sixteen, just like Mack, and had frizzy bright red hair that'd been long overgrown. Accompanying her curls were thousands of freckles, traveling from her forehead down to her neck and arms. She had a younger sister, Maegan (the very same one Noah would watch clouds pass with). Shauna hoisted up an unopened bag of semi-sweet chocolate chips and a frozen bag of brown blueberries, weighing them against each other like a scale. Noah shrugged. Mack had fallen silent; she'd surely gotten over such an important argument.

The other girl, who'd moved to sit on an old sinking couch, was someone Noah recognized, yet he couldn't pin down her name; it sat on the tip of his tongue, but he kept losing it. *Was it Penny? No.... Peggy?* The girl noticed Noah's stare.

"I'm Faye," she said.

Not Peggy.

After taking an agonizingly long time to return the favor, he decided that he'd overstayed his welcome.

* * *

The rest of Noah's morning was spent lying on the living room rug next to Maddy, occasionally leafing through pages of *1984* and sipping on a wide mug of hot chocolate. His mother was in the corner knitting. Sharon had stopped in for a bit to build a cabin from Lincoln Logs. Noah and his mother had helped. Sharon left her construction on the shelf above the fireplace, right in the middle, replacing the wreath that'd been there only a few nights before. She'd given strict instructions to her helpers that it wasn't to be taken apart or moved. Having not gone outside for two days now, Noah grew as restless as Percy. He got up onto his feet and walked on the deep colored maroon rug over to the windowsill. The sky had cleared since he'd woken up. Before, there'd been a heap of fluffy clouds filling up each corner; but now, suddenly, like magic, it was a bluebird day.

Despite the temperatures not wavering so much from yesterday, Noah had decided that it was time to follow in Samuel's galumphing footsteps and go outside. He made his way into the kitchen, past the girls, and into the mudroom to assemble. Noah's snow pants and coat had been Mack's before his, and although he wasn't ecstatic about the neon purple jacket, it'd always kept him toasty. After spending some five minutes searching for his left mitten, Noah was one step away from venturing out from the house and into the Thredsum tundra. Reaching down between his legs, he slid out a basket and pulled out a fresh addition. For his birthday last May, Noah had been given a pair of his own Bean Boots. In his weeks prior to becoming a teenager, Noah had gone to school with his father's pair, stumbling his way from class to class. His new pair were chocolate brown, just like Maddy, and had a steel toe at the end of them. They also weren't a size thirteen. Noah double knotted the yellow strings, got himself up, and turned the knob. With a click, the door cracked open, allowing a sliver of cold air to sneak into unfamiliar quarters. It took only one, maybe two steps in his yard before snow had caved into Noah's boots. His feet still felt plenty warm. With a shrug, he walked his way over to Samuel's footsteps, meticulously placing each step in the craters his brother had made.

Left, right, left, right.

It took Noah a half an hour to reach a left-hand turn in the tracks. After a quick surveillance of the land in front of him, the long stretch of shadowed tracks made Noah come to a rather disappointing realization. There would be a lot more walking, and only two more changes of direction. Samuel had made a gigantic circle. Noah had hoped that his brother would've gone into the woods, or maybe across the street. A big circle was boring.

Shelley Avenue, which was parallel to his steps, was as busy as ever. As cars whizzed past him, Noah couldn't help but daydream about the night before. He wondered if he should go back to the big rock and check on the deer's body. He wondered if his ghost would still be there waiting. The snow day had distracted him from thinking about both what he'd seen and sensed, and now that he was thinking, he couldn't help but start and envision the carcass. His thoughts piggybacked on one another until all he could see was the deer's open eye and the dazzlingly dark puddle underneath its body—a symbol of the spirit that stalked behind the tree trunks. He remembered how clean the line between fur and tissue had been; it was as if someone had cut it open with a knife. Noah convinced himself that the deer had most likely fallen on an unlucky stick after being shot by a gamesman; it was then skinned for a trophy and left to rot. Coming to a logical explanation didn't make the scene any less unsettling, though; he could still feel how his body had felt when he'd been in the woods. There'd been a pressure that weighed heavy on his chest—an animalistic reaction that screamed at him with an unquestionable credibility that someone else was there.

A car that whizzed by honked loudly and snapped Noah back into reality. Off across the hills and to his west, he could see the steeple of Woodrow's Church, the tallest point in his town. Hidden just beyond the landmark was one of the town's country stores, a place run by an old man he'd only ever known as 'Sir'. Noah frequented the spot in the summer months for soft drinks and snacks. To the right of the steeple were the rolling hills that belonged to a nature conservatory. The sky had turned into a shade close to the color of his coat, and what had to be the slimmest crescent moon Noah had ever seen was emerging over faraway branches; it was turned on its side, and faintly beamed down on him like a ghostly smile. His feet felt cold, and he was getting hungry. In search of a granola bar, he checked all the pockets he had on him, but could only find a Ken Griffey Jr. baseball card that he thought he'd lost a while back. He put the card back in his coat pocket, turned around, and stepped back into his own tracks.

Left, right, left, right.

The car that'd beeped at him earlier had turned around and pulled over beside him, this time returning with a much louder honk than the one before. It wasn't a good-looking car by any means; the front bumper hung just inches from the ground, the doors had rusted over, and the little hatch that opened for gas was nonexistent. Shauna yelled out of the half-opened passenger side window and over the hum of a clunking engine for Noah to get in the car 'or else'. The coldness in his feet outweighed the surefire headache he'd have in twenty minutes, and, reluctantly, Noah climbed over the low wooden fence and made his way into the car.

Noah stopped thinking about the deer as soon as the car moved, as he was preoccupied in trying to figure out how in the world Faye had passed her driver's test. At one point she went (maximum) fifteen miles per hour up a straightaway hill, and then minutes later she was pushing (minimum) forty on a downhill. At last, they met up with the low wooden fence. Noah could see his home up ahead. He never knew his toes could be as excited as they were then.

The old Buick was making way towards its destination at an alarming speed. The turn was only thirty feet away now. Faye only sped up. And then, she screamed past the driveway, driving until the soft yellow lights of the Libby home were out of Noah's view. Mack prodded him.

"Dinner at Shaun's."

V

THE Murphy's house wasn't nearly as big as Noah's. Despite it being much smaller, Noah and Mack both preferred the house to their own. The front entrance to the home stepped onto an indoor porch, enclosed in several panels of windows. It faced east, and in the mornings the room would turn golden. On Mack's final day of elementary school, she and Noah had gone over to Shauna and Maegan's for breakfast before biking to school together. That morning, they ate toasted banana bread with butter for breakfast (Mack's favorite) and watched the sunrise.

Noah followed Shauna, Faye, and Mack inside the porch, up some steps, and then through a second door. The second door swung open to reveal the largest room in the house; it was at least half the size of Noah's own living room, with a fireplace on its far side and two couches pushed closely together on an extremely frayed rug. The shelf above the fireplace had at least fifteen pictures crammed on its surface, all fighting for space with Christmas decorations that still hadn't been taken down. Emmylou (the eldest of the two Murphy cats) lounged on the ground between the two couches that filled the room. The girls had taken off their boots and were stacking them on top of one another near the doorway. The room was quite warm, and although Noah couldn't tell exactly what was being cooked, aromatic smells of buttery pastries and meaty stew came from the next room over.

The sky was getting dark. Noah could just barely see the backyard out the window to his left, but he knew that cloaked in the deep blues and purples of the outside was a beautiful garden; it was structured around pathways lined with stones, weaving as a narrow dirt passage in the summer months between fields of lilies and raspberry bushes. The path led to a wall of green and yellow, with sunflowers (which, from below, appeared to be three times the size of a middle schooler) bunched together to create a forest of sorts. Inside its walls, the path continued until it reached a hidden alcove, surrounded by stalks and vines, and with a flat stone in its center used as a reading seat. When the sun would shine, the dirt inside would glow as green as the stalks that surrounded it; and when the sun got tired, the path was always the first of the entire yard to be met with the night. The visuals that danced in Noah's head were drenched in memories of the summertime, but now it was the beginning of winter. The rocks that lined the path were now tiny hills of snow, and the fields and forest that once ruled the yard were now just dead dirt underneath a white blanket.

As Noah looked down to unlace his boots, the girls migrated around a corner and up the home's only flight of stairs. His hands buzzed from the sudden heat of the house, and he could feel the ice on his feet melt into a puddle. Upon taking off his boots, he found his socks were soaked through. When he pinched his big toe all he could feel was pressure. His mittens, snow pants, hat, and socks were now either hanging from or draped over a scalding hot radiator. Soon after he'd stacked his boots above everyone else's, a fast *tap tap tap tap tap tap tap* came down the staircase. A girl of the same height and age as Noah swung around the corner and ran towards him; her long, unkempt brunette hair flew from side to side.

"Noah!"

Upon the impact of a big hug, Noah could feel his cheeks turn pink and his ears burn slightly; he'd developed a massive crush on Maegan last summer but was still a long way away from telling her any of the feelings he had. For now, he was more than fine with having her as just a friend (or so he told himself several times).

"Come on," she continued excitedly, "I've *gotta* show you something!"

"Is it outside?" Noah asked apathetically (though he hid his frown behind a well-timed nose-scratch). A quick turn and rush back towards the stairs answered his question right away. He jogged after her before he had a chance to take off his jacket, trying his best to keep up with Maegan's pace, hopping up three steep steps at a time in order not to lose her (*although it would be hard to lose someone in such a small house*, Noah thought to himself). Emmylou followed right on Noah's heels. Maegan had taken a left and gone into the bathroom across the hall from her bedroom. After beckoning him in, she shut the door behind Noah and the cat.

"Just watch," she whispered as she squished her way past him. Maegan was crouched down in between the sink and the toilet, looking closely at the bricks that made up the bathroom's wall, her freckled nose an inch away. Noah always found it funny that only one side of the bathroom had brick showing. The rest of the bathroom's surroundings were covered in baby blue polka dotted wallpaper.

"Here!"

Maegan pulled out a loose brick from the wall as if she was playing a game of Jenga. She did this twelve more times, each time placing the bricks on the seat of the toilet next to her. Noah noticed that Maegan had drawn small X's on the front of each of them. After withdrawing a dusty flashlight from her pullover, she leaned into the small hole in the wall. As soon as she pointed the light in, she let out a breath of excitement as if she'd discovered a room full of gold and silver.

"Look, Noah! Look inside!"

He crouched himself down, and, following Maegan's strict instructions, pointed the flashlight she'd given him into the hole in the wall.

Noah wouldn't call what he was staring at a room of any sorts. Maybe a burrow, but even that seemed generous. A bright white rock in the corner blinded Noah when he shined he light its way. Divergent in appearance from the dark brick that surrounded it, he deduced that the rock must've been put there by Maegan himself. Aside from the stone, the spot was an empty little space. It stretched maybe two feet in width and height and looked remarkably clean. Finding any unseen area in a house so small was still astonishing, make no mistake. However, Noah wasn't anywhere near Maegan's level of elation.

"This is our spot," Maegan boasted.

A sudden knock at the door caused Emmylou to jump up from the floor and into the hole in the wall.

"We're brushing our teeth!" yelled Maegan in the hallway's direction, not a moment of hesitation in her speech.

"What?!" yelled back Shauna from the other side of the bathroom door. Noah couldn't help but slip into a fit of laughter. Maegan nudged his rib to get him to stop. He covered his mouth.

"I said that we're brushing our teeth!"

No response. Shauna had walked down the hall and gone back into her room.

"Anyway," said Maegan with a shrug, "you and I can put all sorts of things in here and no one will know!"

Noah paused for a second, not knowing what to say. He hated having to fabricate his feelings, especially for Maegan.

"Cool!"

"*Just* cool?"

"Yeah, it's really cool."

Noah noticed Maegan's cheeks go pink with embarrassment. Emmylou watched from her booth.

"I just thought you'd be into it."

"I am!"

"Are you?"

"I swear I am."

"What would you put inside it then?"

Maegan's hands were crossed over her chest. Noah knew he had to think of an answer quickly; he looked down at his shoes.

"Clothes maybe?"

"*Clothes?*"

"Yeah, so you could, you know.... free up other space."

Noah looked up after he spoke, and upon seeing her face he instantaneously recognized the mistake he'd made. She was chewing the side of her lip furiously and her head shook in short little bursts.

"No! Not clothes!" she snapped in a loud whisper. "I know I don't live in a farmhouse with gigantic closets and guest rooms like *some people*, but that doesn't mean I'm fighting with my family for storage spaces!"

Noah opened his mouth to return with another poorly thought-out response, but Maegan had begun again before he was given the chance to say anything.

"*Listen*," she hissed, "I want to put journals, and pieces of sea glass, and receipts, and coins, and rocks, and notes, and drawings, and whatever else that I find in here. Not my *sweaters*!"

It was after saying this that Maegan's face had turned away and gone bright red. Noah had given up; she sounded genuinely hurt.

"I'm sorry," he said, fidgeting with one of the several bricks Maegan had put on the toilet.

She paused for a few moments, then opened her mouth, then paused again. Noah could see the battle she was having with herself—an internal debate on whether to accept his apology or not. While Maegan worked to find her words, Emmylou climbed out of the wall and started scratching at the knob on the bathroom door.

"I don't accept your apology, but—" she said, looking up at him, "—but I'd feel better if you'd tell me you understand what I want the spot for."

Noah nodded his head at top speed. Maegan answered back

with a half-smile. He rummaged through his pants pockets for anything at all, even a coin or two, but all he could feel were crumbs and a few pieces of lint. Running out of options, he reached into his coat pocket and felt it: sharp, square, and thin.

"This is a baseball card my aunt gave me a while back."

"I thought you just had uncles?" she asked, her eyes lit up with a rush of curiosity.

"Well, I never really got to meet her," he said while looking at the hole in the wall, afraid to glance in Maegan's direction.

"Oh."

"Anyway, it's really important to me. I'd like to keep it here if that's okay."

She nodded, looking much less annoyed than she was only a minute ago. Instead, she looked somewhat sorrowful. A call came from below, so the two of them finally left the bathroom and went downstairs.

* * *

After dinner had ended, Noah and Maegan found their way back into the living room, now balmy from a fire the latter had revived. Shauna, Faye, and Mack soon joined them. Everyone had stretched out on the couches, full of Mrs. Murphy's minced pies and cinnamon rolls. While his sister and her friends were discussing 'grown-up things' (SATs, prom, *Gilmore Girls*, etc.),

Noah was busy helping Maegan pick out lint that was stuck to the side of Bo, the smaller and scruffier of the Murphy's cats.

"I really have no clue how he gets like this," said Maegan while she pulled out a sizable ball of red wool from Bo's side. "He stays inside all day."

Although Noah felt more guilty with time, he forced himself to be interested in Bo's indoor habits as much as possible, refraining from scratching a fiery itch to discuss the unwisely guess he'd made for what belonged in the secret space in Maegan's bathroom wall. On top of it all, he also felt awful for telling her the baseball card was a gift from his late aunt. He didn't even have an aunt. The time had passed to tell her the truth—it would only make things messier.

"Maybe he was in your sister's hair," Noah suggested. Maegan let out a giggle and then subsequently closed one eye, pinched the wool in between her index finger and thumb, and looked across the room at her sister.

"I think you've finally found out what Bo's been up to all these nights. I guess Shaun's hair makes a nice little duvet."

After thirty or so minutes of pointless conversations (which mostly held Mack making fun of Noah and Maegan being alone in the bathroom), Faye announced she ought to get home sooner rather than later. While Shauna and Maegan made their way upstairs to start their homework, Noah snuck his way back into the kitchen to thank their mother for dinner. Mrs. Murphy sat in the kitchen's corner on a table that encapsulated the style of her house; it was exceptionally small and extremely low to the ground, with a circular wooden surface that was on an axis so crooked that if an orange was placed on it, it would roll off and fall flat onto the floor. She hadn't noticed Noah's stare, let alone that he'd entered the kitchen.

Mrs. Murphy, just like her eldest daughter, had vibrant red hair before it'd greyed. She was short, and, as Noah had heard her say, 'big boned, not pudgy.' he constantly wore scarves and sweaters that she'd knit herself; tonight's wardrobe involved a dark green sweater with what looked like a badly sewn deer on it. She was a single mother to Shauna and Maegan for as long as Noah had known their family. It wasn't uncommon for her to invite Mack and him over for dinner. Besides his own mother, she was truly the warmest and sweetest woman that he'd ever known.

That night, Mrs. Murphy looked as nice and calm as always, wholly invested in whatever thoughts were circling around in her head. Papers were spread out all over the crooked wood surface and her face was bent over the batch. The tip of her clog clicked itself against a wooden peg like a metronome—tapping, tapping, tapping.

Instead of nosing around like he'd done with the deer, he decided to leave the kitchen and go put on his jacket. His socks now warm and dry, Noah slipped into his boots and gingerly shut the door.

VI

NOAH ate his dry and cold supper by himself, sitting on the sinking couch where Faye had been yesterday. His plate was on his knees and his utensils kept falling from it and onto the wooden kitchen floor. It didn't take long for him to swipe the remains from his plate into the Insinkerator. The day had felt as though it was the length of two. Morning was a distant memory.

He'd gone the whole previous night dawdling and forgot the test he had in the morning, only to remember as his alarm rang, and it was much too late to start any studying. It'd felt like he'd only just shut his eyes; the sounds of the house settling down were just ringing his ears—creaking and gurgling around his dark room.

The crescent moon was gone, and the dull winter sky had faintly lit up the mess on his floor. He shot up out of his bed and rushed over to his bureau, grabbed clothes at random, ignoring the fact that he'd put his socks on inside out. He skipped making any adjustments in front of his grand mirror. Instead, he knelt on his floorboards and compiled all the books he'd neglected to read, opening all of them to their last pages. After reading for a few minutes, Noah noticed his stomach rumble. Page after page he read, ignoring the shouts from downstairs telling him that he was going to be late. Although his eyes scanned from line to line, he could only think about how stressed he was, about how he was going to not know a single thing, about how stupid he was for neglecting his work. *Rose of Sherry, is it? No.... Sharon.... think of your sister.... Rose and Sharon.... Right?*

He gave up cramming after the eighth call from his mother and sprinted to the kitchen. He had no time to eat breakfast, let alone assemble one, nor check if everything he needed was in his schoolbag. When he made it to the mudroom, he groaned at the realization he still had to lace up his boots. As they were still damp from yesterday, he instead slipped on his sneakers and raced his way outside. The weather matched his mood with gray, overcast skies and a drizzle of freezing rain. He reached the street as soon as the big yellow school bus pulled over.

Both Sharon and Samuel had left on a bus before him, and Mack was waiting to be picked up by Faye or some other friend. Noah was the only member of his family in middle school, awkwardly stuck between adolescence and independence. He worked his way to the back of the bus and swung himself down next to the farthest window, leaning his bag against the back hatch. Maegan always sat by the window on the other side; the back row had no aisle, so it stretched all the way across. That morning, she was nowhere to be seen. Noah immediately pulled out the novels from his bag and began skimming.

He'd felt in the past that eighth grade was moving slower than most school years, however nothing had dragged on quite like the next six hours. He was uncharacteristically irritable from the moment he'd shut *To Kill a Mockingbird* and stepped off the bus.

First block came and went in what felt like four hours. The test went as poorly as Noah had feared it would. He was the last one to hand his sheet in, scribbled with vague answers and eraser marks out the wazoo. After he'd taken his walk of shame back to his desk, Mr. McKinley, his English teacher with a special talent of speaking in a monotonous way, had announced that he along with all other eighth-grade teachers would soon write performance reviews for every student; they'd assess each student's ability to persevere in their work, respect one another, and exhibit 'responsible characteristics'. Every day, Mr. McKinley would jot down a word-of-the-day on the chalkboard. Ironically, today it was 'nihilism'.

Mr. McKinley's tired mentioning that the evaluations were being sent to high school teachers was met with a shared panic that caused several heads to spin around and ears to perk up. Before anyone could ask for more specifics, Mr. McKinley waved the back of his hand in a way that motioned the class period had ended. Noah felt a headache come on in the front of his skull while the classroom filled with the sounds of squeaking footsteps and hushed concerns. Stress had turned him introverted; he didn't even notice his closest school friends, Warren Walker and Sam Barnaby, enter or leave the classroom.

As Noah moved his way upstairs for social studies, he noticed that the drizzle of freezing rain had transitioned into a steady fall. Pellets popped viciously against windows lining the staircase that he ran up. Social studies was a bit better than English, but he still felt like it lasted twice its normal length. The teacher, Mrs. Hannings, was one of his favorites; and the subject, World War II, was particularly of his interest. Despite this, Noah still found ways to be frustrated throughout the period. He'd spent most of his time in class zoned out, remembering how Mack had spent the entire ride home last night commenting on how horrible Noah was at flirting. Science class also moved like molasses, and lunch with Warren and Sam was even slower. Sam was tall and skinny; he had dark hair and a mouth that always hung open. His voice was low and soft. In contrast, Warren was smaller than Sam but taller than Noah. He was buff for his age and had platinum blonde hair. His raspy voice was still catching up to his body, though. Sam had spent the first half of the period pestering Warren into telling him the answer to a riddle.

"Yeah, yeah, but why do *you* get to go through the green glass door?"

During the latter half of the block, the two argued on whether or not a peck counted as a kiss. Warren got defensive.

"You haven't gotten either so don't talk."

Even gym class took longer than usual. Noah had gone into class hoping they would be playing something fun to close out the school day. Instead of playing floor hockey, though, he sat on a yoga mat, scribbling in little bubbles on a state issued Physical Education survey. All the mats were musky, emitting a similar scent to that of a pair of old jeans left out in a rainstorm, and the room was too cold to be comfortable. 'Professor' Giles sat in his office, filling in a crossword. Noah noticed he had a stain, a red splotch the size of a silver dollar that sat next to the collar of his Izod. Set in the curving and neon frame of golden arches, he imagined him taking a sharp turn in his truck and a ketchup-dipped hash brown falling.

When the bell had finally rung, Noah lazily made his way over to the office to place his sheet down on top of the others. He exited the back door and walked up to the big semicircle drop-off zone where his bus waited for him. In the center of the circle stood a big and ugly statue shaped in the bulbus form of the school's founding principal, Augustus Rulch. Raindrops splattered off his bald bronze head and puddled at his feet. Noah got on the bus quickly, as to avoid getting his sneakers more soaked than they already were. Just like he'd done in the morning, he glanced from seat to seat as he walked down the narrow aisle. Maegan was again absent. He swung his way into the same place he'd sat to skim books.

The drive home, like his classes, was painfully long. Soon after the first stop, one of the front tires had blown out, causing a thirty-minute pit stop on the side of a narrow street. While the driver was outside fixing the blown tire, everyone on board had raised their volume three-fold. The clamor made Noah's headache grow considerably, and no matter how many times he adjusted his position he couldn't find a comfy place to rest his head. Later, as the bus huffed up Shelley Avenue, he turned and looked out the window, which now was covered in dashes of cold water. He had hopes that he'd see his tracks from yesterday afternoon, but everything had turned to mush, and he couldn't make anything out.

Dinner was appropriately leftovers. The mashed potatoes Noah had heated in the microwave were chalky and cold in the middle, and the meatloaf he ate with it was dry as wood. Noah's father was out working his winter job of collecting kindling and firewood to sell, and his mother had eaten an early dinner. Sharon and Samuel had joined her. Mack was up in her room and talking loudly on the phone. Thus, Noah ate his dry and cold supper by himself, sitting on the sinking couch where Faye had been yesterday. His plate was on his knees, his utensils kept falling off and onto the wooden kitchen floor, and it didn't take long for him to swipe the remains from his plate into the Insinkerator.

Noah walked his way back to his room in a similarly lackadaisical way to when he'd turned in his P.E exam. As he crossed into the heart of the house, he heard Sharon and Samuel in the playroom whisper about something they found amusing. They tried to hush out the conversation at the sight of their older brother.

"Sharpoo, *no*! don't tell! You can't!" Samuel whispered to his sister, holding both her shoulders to prevent her from turning.

"But he —"

"No!" cried Samuel. Sharon looked befuddled. Noah laughed and moved on. He wished he could spend his evenings playing around until he wore himself out, and he fantasized of what it would be like to not have to worry about tests, or performance reviews, or girls.

Upon entering his room, he noticed the moon trying to peek out from behind clouds that wandered by. He could make out that it was marginally bigger than the night before. It looked like a banana. With a quick flick, he turned the lamp on his bedside table on. At the sound of the switch, the room was instantly illuminated with soft golden light. The added stress of performance reviews had triggered Noah to start his homework without his usual doodling (although, a thought *did* pop into his head that he could showcase perseverance by starting the evaluation period by not doing any work, and then progressively doing more until he received better grades in the weeks to come). After an hour of struggling with his math homework, he began leafing through an introduction he'd been given to read for English. Not long after he began reading, he'd given up and assured himself that there would be enough time tomorrow evening to finish.

Noah soon returned from the bathroom with wet hair and clean teeth. He swung into his room on sliding socks and jumped into his bed as if he was a center fielder making a diving catch (its covers had been neatly reset by his mother or father) He propped two big fluffed up pillows vertically against his bed frame before resting his back against them. Next to the glowing lamp sat Noah's book, which he swiped up from its spot, replacing it with a tall glass of water he'd filled up in the bathroom.

He promptly started reading, opening onto a page with a cut down straw of hay that acted as a bookmark. He'd read this specific story many times now (the name of the book doesn't matter, although it is worth noting that it couldn't have been any more different from *The Grapes of Wrath*). Noah sat still for three chapters, testing how long he could read without having to make a much-needed trip to the bathroom. Eventually, he surrendered. Upon returning to from his pee, he put his empty glass on the floor and his marked book back to its spot beside the light. With another flick, the room went fully dark.

No matter how many times he'd shifted which side he laid on, he couldn't seem to get comfortable. A thousand thoughts were zooming left and right through his head like the cars outside on Shelley Avenue. He could acknowledge one at a time, but the constant rush of ideas and memories blocked him from unpacking anything specific. His imaginations spoke in voices, too—ones that sounded like his own; it was a cacophony of sounds, all madly flying around, none of which were able to be identified. The house settled around him similarly to the night before. Pipes began gargling, floorboards were loudly setting themselves into the house, and wood on the walls creaked. The sounds could only contrast themselves against the deluge of imaginary noises in Noah's head.

As he laid on his right shoulder, and as random reflections spun themselves behind his closed eyelids, a hiss came from his hallway. His eyes shot wide open; his ears perked like a hunting dog's. All the imaginations that'd been moving around in his head had vanished, his mind now fully focused on what he thought he'd just heard. He sat up on his bed, legs crossed over one another and his head tilted towards his propped door. He sat and listened as hard as he possibly could. Silence. Not even a heating pipe had made a sound since he'd sat up. And then, he heard the deep moan of Fredrick's cello, hauntingly quiet and beautiful. It stopped only a few notes in, though—his father surely had come downstairs to tell him to stop; it was much too late to be playing.

He sat still for a few more minutes, crisscrossed, only moving his fingers to pull out a loose string that hung from his t-shirt. And then, out of the quiet darkness, the same peculiar noise that'd shot Noah up returned.

The sound was unmistakable this time around. Hushed whispers came from what sounded like only ten feet away, and as faint as they were, the sounds traveled easily through the ambience. It sounded like the voice of a little boy, and although Noah hadn't the slightest clue what the little boy was saying, he could distinguish through tone that it was something of importance. After a quick pinch on the thigh, he recapped what had happened and rationalized his thoughts. *It must be Samuel.... He was saying something to Sharon earlier....*

The room was still dark as ever, but for some odd reason Noah's eyes had still not fully adjusted yet. He quietly reached his way over to the light to turn it on, surely to expose his little brother with his hands cupped on the door. His arms swung blindly, a mad attempt to find the table while keeping his eyes set on the dark hall.

A sudden boom echoed around the room. The book that was once on the bed stand had fallen flat onto the floor. He ruffled around in his covers to lean down and pick it up, creating a flurry of sounds that blocked all others out. Upon reaching for the book, his hand clipped the top of the glass he'd put down, knocking it on its side and shattering it into a thousand pieces. He whipped his head toward his table and switched on his lamp. Tiny shards had gone to the north, south, east, and west of his bedroom. Glass was in his strewn clothes, near the wall underneath his window, underneath his bed—everywhere.

He swept the sharp pieces up with the cover of the book that'd fallen to the floor. Once he'd finished, his pile of broken glass bounced the lamp's golden light around like a great big gold medallion. It took a few minutes to clean up, and by the time he'd dumped the shards into his trash can it seemed that his brother had fled the scene. After a few more minutes of quiet listening, Noah fell back into his bed. Going after him wasn't worth his time. He reached across his body to turn off the light again.

He was restless now; it was impossible to prevent him from imagining what would've happened if he swung out from his bed and slipped his feet into slippers. In his mind, he'd already made his way across the house, eventually reaching the sounds of Samuel's giggles. He'd be in Mack's room with Sharon. Upon entry, things would've seemed suspicious. Mack would be reading aloud a book to the two youngest, but they'd be distracted, clearly much more interested in something that they both found to be hilarious. Noah pictured himself asking them to not bug him like that again. They would've visibly broken out into laughter, and Mack would've tried to hide her own.

As he curled up again and thought about the various ways he could confront his siblings, he couldn't help but remember what his mother had told him. Why was he supposed to forgive someone who was always so mean? He didn't care about Mack's schoolwork, let alone her search for the perfect university. She treated him, he thought, like someone who was dumb, who understood nothing, who always needed their hand held. At that moment, he made himself believe he was ready for middle school to end and for high school to begin. The sounds of pipes, floorboards, and walls occasionally croaking and creaking came and went like before. This time, however, the voice was gone. Noah had soon fallen into a deep sleep before he could think of any more ways to get his revenge. Later, the box with the sleigh bells and his grandmother's letter had heard sounds he wouldn't hear for many nights to come.

VII

JANUARY and February's weather continued to be as desolate as it was the day Noah had failed his English test; clouds were constantly clumped together in the air and were indiscernible from one another. Masses of gray hung in the air for so many days that it seemed oddly foreign when blue sky had finally poked its way through. Before the weather had shifted, the winter months felt like they'd last forever, trapping all of Somerset County in a purgatorial state of freezing rain and sleet.

Noah wasn't sad to see the winter weather dissipate; he'd spent most days cooped up with homework that towered over him and expectations which tirelessly treaded around in his head. February was an especially terrible month; all the teachers were constantly jotting down notes whenever someone spoke out without raising their hand, or talked to a neighbor, or even chewed gum too loudly.

During lunch, it would be normal to catch entire tables in deep discussion about grades. Noah could always hear worried voices in the cafeteria dooming themselves to future failure. It seemed like most of Noah's peers were less worried about being considered an 'honor' student than they were about the potential of a split in their social lives. High school was fast approaching, and as excited as Noah was for more freedom, he wasn't looking forward to the hours of readings and the pressures that would come with fitting in. *And what about college?* Although he was still bitter towards her, Noah felt a bit pitiful for Mack.

During one weekend, only a few days after students had passed out valentine candies to one another, Noah didn't leave his house once. Friday, Saturday, and Sunday had been indistinguishable from one another; for the clouds had no depth to them and rained and snowed in the same wintry mix. The only Libby child that dared to go outside was Samuel. On Friday, during a common rainy-day game of hide and seek with Sharon and Noah, he'd camped out underneath the wrap-around porch for a half hour—a loophole to the rule of staying inside the house, as he'd 'not *really* gone out-of-bounds'. Unlike the mudroom in which his siblings were searching in, the ground beneath it was poorly insulated, and Samuel hadn't brought any layers but the ones he wore (being only a crewneck and sweatpants). Only a handful of hours after surrendering to Mother Nature, he'd come down with mild cold symptoms. The first wave came after dinner on Friday, when he'd started sneezing in between telling his father how he'd outsmarted his siblings. When Saturday breakfast rolled around, he was quick to renounce the hiding spot, as it resulted in a fit of morning sniffles and a throat so sore that he could hardly suck on cough drops. His mother cared for him all of Saturday; from sun-up to sun-down she brought him tea and cookies and read to him, disregarding the work calls she had to make and the orders she had to finalize.

That same night, Noah had gone up to see Samuel in hopes of wishing him good health before he turned in. Unsurprisingly, his mother was there, tucked under the covers and with Samuel's little head resting on her shoulder; his eyes were closed, and he was breathing heavily from his mouth. His cheeks were flushed, and his nose was bright red. Hundreds of tissues were crumpled into two separate waste baskets at the foot of the twin sized bed. The other bed was empty—a distant mumbling revealed Sharon to be in the room across the hall, getting a bedtime story read to her by her father. Noah's mother had instantly noticed him peek into the room. She smiled at his coming.

"He's doing okay," she said softly out towards the doorway where the elder of her two sons stood. Noah nodded.

"Has he been blowing his nose at all?" he whispered with an air of comedy. She laughed an inaudible laugh and nodded back. He took a long look at his little brother, who looked so at peace that the watcher's heart couldn't help but be warmed. Upon shifting his stare back at his mother, he knew that Samuel would be recovered come Sunday morning. Her heart was as good as gold, and that was the best medicine anyone could receive.

* * *

About two and a half months after Samuel Libby had manifested a snow day came a remarkably warm Wednesday. Whether for better or for worse, the performance reviews had been signed, sealed, and delivered just before the temperatures rose. Late March had come, and stress, like snow, had melted into shallow puddles in anticipation for springtime. In the time that elapsed, Noah's father had pitched their blueberries to markets in downtown Portland, while his mother had been working on a similar project with shops in Northern New Hampshire.

At dawn, the air was already heavy with fifty-degree breezes that drifted in from the faraway coast. Chickadees twittered about in the big elm tree while Robins closely surveyed the dead grass below.

Light had woken Noah up before his alarm could. After a rub of his eyes and a stretch of his arms, he stepped out of bed to open his window—something he hadn't done in many months. On his way over, he tripped on his nightstand, knocking the book he loved onto the wood floor. Upon opening the window, he was greeted with birds chirping and warm winds—both which encouraged and ultimately convinced him to wear shorts for the first time that year; it was a choice Noah would later find many of his peers had also made.

If any Mainer was randomly dropped in front of the walkway leading up into Thredsum Middle School, they'd most likely think it was June (possibly May). Almost every single student had shorts and a t-shirt on, with a good portion of them locking their bikes up on a rack outside the school. A football was being thrown around as well as a frisbee or two; for no one was in a rush to swing open the big oak doors and start their first block classes. Noah had taken the bus, as usual, but after he stepped out into the schoolyard, he decided that he'd walk home come afternoon.

As he made his way over the sunny yard, he dug around in his shorts pockets to check if he'd grabbed everything he'd planned on bringing with him. To his pleasure, oddly enough, he felt a rusted coin and the tip of an arrowhead rub against his fingers. Ever since Maegan had shown him the hidden spot in her bathroom, which she'd dubbed 'Emmy's Hollow', a reference to her favorite cat's reverence for the spot, the two had been adding items every week, whether it be drawings Maegan had sketched on the school bus or smoothed rocks Noah had discovered around the farm. It only took a few days after dropping his baseball card in for Noah to pass along more souvenirs, trinkets, and findings—all things his parents claimed to be trash. He'd adopted the habit of stashing whatever into his back pocket, as long as it was little enough to fit and would make him think a bit deeper about something.

During the weeks that followed the snow day in early January, Noah had designated the bottom right corner of his closet as an area where he could temporarily store all his findings. To him, they were nothing short of tangible memories, journaled in secret and surrounded by an ocean of what Maegan and him collectively and quietly agreed was the adult world.

The hollow housed pennies and bottle caps and shoestrings and hats, along with necklaces and rings and beads and popsicle sticks glued together and painted over; tiny oblong ceramic bowls and bunches of wire sat on brick shelves inside the walls, too. A bundle of papers, eight pages thick, sat atop the pile. Its edges were curled (a lasting result of once being rolled up in a tight tube) and was strapped in a frayed yellow cord of twine. Written in his difficult-to-read handwriting was a story Noah was too shy to share with Warren, Sam, or even his mother or father. Even though Maegan had said she wouldn't read it, Noah wished she would. She wouldn't have to tell him she had. He actually preferred that. He was weak that way.

Noah wasn't thinking about any of that now. After scribbling down a memory of being beaten up in the fourth grade, he'd put it away and hadn't looked at what he'd written.

In fact, he hadn't thought about the day at all. He didn't feel like he needed to anymore.

Sam waited for him at the doors, wearing baggy pinstripe shorts and a Boston Celtics t-shirt that was much too small for him. The previous summer, Noah had been close to if not the same height as him. In the months since vacation, though, Sam had shot up at least half a foot; on most days you could see his belt and a good portion of his ankles. He'd already outgrown his older brother, John, who was so opposite from him that it was comical. John was in the same year as Mack and was similarly sharp and exceedingly snobby, while Sam had more of a relaxed attitude towards things.

Sam stood on the steps alone while others began filtering past him. Katie Ross and Georgia Winnings, two close friends of Maegan's, waved in Sam's direction as they went up the front steps, which triggered Sam to return with a gangly wave that reminded Noah of an inflated tube he'd seen outside of the Thredsum car dealership last week. Warren's absence had most definitely something to do with Drew Carlin, a tall and beautiful dark-haired girl he'd started dating around Christmas time. Before they had the opportunity to greet one another with anything more than a wave, the ring of a bell echoed out onto the schoolyard and students began piling their way inside.

VIII

THE warm weather didn't just have a merry effect on the students of Thredsum Middle School. In Noah's first class of the day, Mrs. Hannings had assigned everyone to pair up with someone of their choice to quiz one another on key American moments from the 1960s. While chairs and tables shuffled themselves around, Mrs. Hannings had put on a bulky set of headphones and closed her eyes to the sounds of bossa nova. Although Noah had his textbook open in front of him, he instead decided to listen to Sam's not-so-well thought out plan of stealing alcohol from his parents; it piqued Noah's interest far more than the moon landing.

"Just think about it, No', drinking a little and adding some water back to it after wouldn't change the color at all."

Prof. Giles was also in an exceptionally cheerful mood. For

the first time since October, the class ventured outside. A profusion of sports balls was thrown on a patch of muddy ground where a soccer field was once discernible, and he gave the class an hour to do whatever they wanted with them. Noah noticed Maegan (who, in his eyes, was looking awfully cute in a peach-colored sundress) and a few of her friends take a soccer ball into a corner of the field. Emmy's Hollow had made the two grow closer over the past weeks; the feelings he'd locked shut were now bubbling up. While Noah thought of creative conversation starters, Warren had already ran to a spot he'd claimed for a game.

* * *

In the sixth and final inning of his Wiffle ball game, Noah could feel his back cling to his striped t-shirt. If his mother had told him it'd been fifty degrees this morning, there was no way, he thought, that the thermostat hadn't now shot past seventy.

"Let's go, Libby!" cried Warren, who'd shuffled a generous lead from Kevin Ricker's shoe—a chunky Reebok which doubled as second base.

Noah stepped up to the plate. The game was tied, and everyone, like Noah, was visibly dripping with sweat. Despite there being no audience, a palpable sense of competitiveness drifted in the humid air. Warren clapped and shuffled his feet to distract the pitcher. Rudy, the first baseman, (his real name was Roger Tellenpope, but no one dared calling him that to his face) muttered obscene comments under his breath to try and distract Noah. Sam waited in the on-deck circle, while Brian Dotty, a boy Sam despised, annotated the scene to death in anticipation of the next pitch (Brian had labeled himself as the commentator in the second inning—a consolation to being asked to sit out so the teams could have even numbers). The six middle schoolers had no audience besides themselves, yet the collective intensity made the game feel like the seventh of the World Series. While Kevin wound up to pitch, a cry from across the field blew the play dead.

Just beyond the corner where Maegan was playing soccer, Katie Ross was walking back inside the school, shaking badly and crying into her arms. The short and stubby right hand of Mrs. Jennings stretched around Katie's shoulder and patted her gently. Noah instantly knew something bad had happened; Mrs. Jennings was the school's guidance counselor, and the only time Noah had seen her outside of her office was when she had to tell a seventh-grade boy that his father had been arrested.

Katie was nowhere to be seen at lunch, and so the tables around Noah, Sam, and Warren all spun their own stories about what had happened. So far, Katie had apparently been expelled for cheating on a math exam, had been told her family was moving to Florida, and was also going to repeat the eighth grade. Other rumors, ones that Noah didn't want to believe, said that

Katie's mother had died. Warren and Sam had agreed that Katie was most likely moving and quickly transitioned into having a less grim conversation about the abbreviated Wiffle ball game. Noah heard their voices but wasn't listening to what they said. As he nibbled away at his lunch, he wondered whether he'd have that same reaction if he was the one being told his family had decided to move.

After he finished his sandwich, he got up to refill his water bottle; some PB&J had gotten stuck in his throat and was annoying him. As he walked over to the fountain, he reheard all the rumors, and many more, being whispered between groups; the once festive spirit in the hallways had been replaced with something much more somber. Noah had known that Katie was popular, but the collective worrying in the cafeteria showed a level of concern that he wouldn't have expected. As he twisted off his lid and began pressing the button on the bottom of the water fountain, Noah looked scanned the lunch-hall. Maegan wasn't at her usual table, nor anywhere in the cafeteria. Georgia Winnings and a few other girls were gone, too. Noah began thinking of various scenarios, unaware that he'd continued to put more water in his already overflowing bottle. *Maybe someone did die....*

"Hello?"

An extraordinarily small girl Noah had never seen before was waiting behind him in line. Embarrassed, he stopped thinking about tragic rumors involving Katie's family and instead screwed up the top of his water bottle and walked back into the buzzing crowd of voices.

School carried on as usual, and although Noah noticed several of his contemporaries still stressing about the abrupt departure of Katie Ross, fourth block English with Mr. McKinley was a much calmer environment than the cafeteria. In fact, he'd chosen the word-of-the-day to be 'tranquility'. The period was deemed a peer-review-session, where for the entire period Noah and the rest of the class were told to get someone else to read their essays on *Because of Winn-Dixie*, the only book that Mr. McKinley assigned in which Noah truly enjoyed.

The afternoon had proven to be even hotter than the morning; the high ceilings and tall walls began to sweat, and the wooden doors began to stick to their entryways. On the far side of the classroom, all the windows were generously cracked open, letting a gentle tempered breeze weave its way in between and around the desks, chairs, and cabinets. A loud and constant hum of voices allowed each pair of reviewers and reviewees an opportunity to have conversations that strayed far from girls and dogs.

In the back corner of the classroom, near an open window that looked out on what once was a Wiffle ball stadium, sat Noah and Warren, deep in a friendly argument regarding the overall importance of baseball, Warren's spring sport, and track, which was Noah's. Even within the relaxed atmosphere, Noah still couldn't shake the empty seat two rows up from him. Lunch was understandable, but Maegan had never skipped any classes in Noah's memory. Before he could conjure up any more disastrous scenarios, the bell rang, and students raced their way towards the door.

Warren made an immediate right at the bottleneck to find Drew, leaving Noah to follow a stream of khaki shorts that migrated towards the main entrance hall. He fought his way in between groups congregating around lockers and finally found the same oak doors where Sam had waited outside earlier that morning. On Mondays and Wednesdays Sam was getting tutored for math, which meant that unlike this morning, no lanky body would wait for Noah on the steps. Having already decided he was going to walk home, Noah strode across the front lawn en route to the road ahead.

As he got closer to the road, he croaked his head up to see a bright blue sky; not even the tiniest cloud could be seen in the far-off horizon. Upon reaching the road, he turned to look back towards his school. It may just have been his eyes deceiving him, but he could've sworn the muddy grass on the soccer field had turned a shade or two greener since second block. Just as he turned away, he saw a flash of light orange emerge from one of the school's side entrances. After doing a double take, Noah realized he was looking at someone familiar, who was all alone, speed-walking away from the school with their nose pointed down at their toes. After just a moment's hesitation, he began walking with a similar pace towards them.

Noah thought that if he hadn't said her name, they would've surely collided. Maegan stood still for a few seconds, unable to speak. Noah could see she was deep in her thoughts about something; his presence had brought her back in touch with reality. After regathering herself, she broke the silence.

"Are you walking home?"

"Yeah, are you?"

In Noah's mind it didn't seem like a difficult question to answer at all, but Maegan clearly found it to be troublesome. For why she struggled, however, Noah couldn't figure out.

"Yes, I think so," she said slowly, sounding out every syllable.

Without another word, they turned their backs to Thredsum Middle School and started walking back towards Shelley Avenue.

It took the two a while to walk themselves out of the winding suburban roads that surrounded their middle school— a trip chock-full of awkward silences and infrequent conversations. At one point in their journey, they finally reached a puddle at the lowest point of Shelley Avenue—the beginning of a long ascent in the direction of the road's apogee. On their climb, the blacktop had lines of mud streaked across it, and the horizon on which the road peaked was muffled from humidity.

Noah was cautious not to mention anything involving Katie. As curious as he was, he thought it was only right for Maegan to bring it up. However, it didn't seem like that would happen anytime soon. She kept her eyes locked on the bare trees to their left with every glance he took in her direction; her hands were clasped together in front of the waist seam of her peach-colored dress, pinching dead skin off from the corners of her thumbs.

The two soon walked parallel to a long white fence that bordered acres of greening grass and a massive red farmhouse. Noah brought up their lingering report cards, and so they discussed the matter while crows swung down and up across the empty road. The sun was still strong, but along the sides of the sky he spotted puffy clouds, each which took their time to fill the rest of the blueness. For the first time that day, she abandoned her arsenal of "oh's" and "yeah's", and instead spoke in full sentences. Enjoying the change, Noah had no desire to interrupt her rant on the difference between honor roll and high honor roll. Instead, he stared at his dirty sneakers step on the white parking line, imagining that it was a tightrope, hundreds of feet above the ground. It wasn't before long that Noah had looked up and realized his driveway was to his right; the timing was horrible, as Maegan had just begun talking. Noah took his first step off the pavement and onto gravel.

"Would you want to keep walking? I don't wanna go home yet."

Noah contained his excitement in a small nod and stepped back onto the long white line.

About halfway between Maegan and Noah's homes came the bend that Faye had once sped around. Almost certain that their destination was Maegan's house, Noah was surprised to see her cut him off and walk straight into the woods that lined the avenue.

"What's up?" he asked. Maegan didn't care to answer his question; she kept going deeper in the forest, and it didn't look like she was going to turn around.

"Come!" she yelled, keeping her head pointed towards the trees. After waiting for a few seconds on the side of the road, Noah decided to follow Maegan's fluttering sundress into the green.

No matter how many times he'd search for one, Noah couldn't distinguish any patterns in Maegan's steps that would suggest she was following a trail. The bright sun that'd saturated the fields had disappeared behind a dense layer of evergreens, and the absence of light amplified certain sounds that circled around Noah's ears. Squirrels and chipmunks ran all over the place, scaling trees and snapping tiny twigs under their paws. Maegan noisily bushwhacked through dead tree limbs and over small, mossy boulders. A light breeze whistled. Deep in the forest, dead ahead, a low, eerie call echoed off the wood. It sounded strange—lower than bird calls normally were. A mile in, the woods looked the same: dark, impenetrable, and ominous.

"You're *sure* you know where we're going to end up?" asked Noah while his eyes shifted to look behind him.

"For the hundredth time, yes!"

Maegan's tone sounded less of someone who was annoyed and more like that of an animated child. Ever since Noah had ducked his way into the brush, she'd only sped up, accelerating into what not only looked like the heart of the forest, but the heart of the world itself. The wind picked up and the sounds of splitting branches became less isolated. Noah tripped over several roots to try and keep up with Maegan, who was now many meters ahead of him. After one of his larger stumbles (in which his nose was only an inch or two above the dirt), one of his palms had grazed a protruding branch of a spruce tree and split open. He kept going; for the wind was too loud to call ahead and he was too deep in the woods to find his way back to the winding avenue.

Despite his earlier questioning and current condition, he knew deep down that Maegan had a solid sense of where she was going. For as long as he could remember, she had a special connection with the woods around their homes. She always knew the species of trees that waved above them on their summer walks, and she always scolded Noah when he tugged off their ripe leaves. In her bedroom she drew vines and branches on her walls—brown and green lines scribbled with eloquence across chipped white paint.

His right hand started to feel damp and warm when Maegan finally came to a stop. Sunlight hit the front of her body, silhouetting her backside to Noah. A border of branches in her surroundings framed her perfectly; it looked as if an enormous cannon ball had been fired through the boulders, roots, and trees where Maegan stood.

As Noah moved closer, the hole that surrounded her grew larger, and not before long he was staring out onto rapids. Great boulders and long logs stuck out from its rush, defying the laws that forced everything else in it southbound. Some thirty meters away, tall pines rustled on the far side of the river despite there being a noticeable absence of any wind. *Tranquility.*

Somehow, surprisingly, Maegan seemed less excited about this paradisiacal discovery than she did after first showing Noah the hole in the brick wall of her bathroom. Nevertheless, she smiled for the first time since gym class; her thumbs had stopped being picked at, and the anxious fluttering in her eyes had ceased. She'd found some sort of peace in the moment, and so did Noah. It subsided, though, almost as quickly as it came about. Her eyes panned down to her feet similarly to Noah's when he'd been staring at the white line on Shelley Avenue. Not before long, tears were swimming in her sea-green eyes. She pricked at her thumbs again and her lip trembled a bit.

"Katie's mom died this morning."

IX

NATURE stayed indifferent towards the crushing news Maegan delivered. The river water crashed against the worn rocks in the same way it did before. The evergreens were still swaying, the site still serene. Above the sighing pines and some miles away, a lost balloon floated until it became a dot and disappeared. Despite the mentioning of something so tragic, something that made Noah's stomach lurch and his heart race, everything in front of him stayed immutable and invariable as God themself. Still, he held a deep feeling that the gargling current and the waterlogged tree trunks had listened and even understood what had happened; he couldn't explain it, but he knew it to be true. While he reflected, the memory of spotting the gap in the elm tree shot in his mind as if there was some sort of parallel, though he had trouble finding a connection between the two.

On second thought, it seemed foolish to Noah that he'd believed anything around him would've changed after Meaghan told him Katie's mother had died. What did he expect would happen? Would the clouds roll in and cover the sun? Or would the sounds he'd mistaken for wind die down into a murmur? The questions he asked himself made him feel like a blade of grass alongside a million others. The river, the rocks, the trees, and the sun didn't care about Noah, or Maegan, or Katie's mom. They never could.

Maegan's face was now glazed with tears, and although in his brief absence from reality he hadn't remembered how it happened, she was hugging Noah tighter than she ever had. Big blots of tears splashed down on his t-shirt; her hair smelled like grapefruit and honey. The girl that'd constantly made him overanalyze their most mundane conversations was hugging him, yet he didn't get any enjoyment out of it. No blood rushed to his cheeks, no sweating, no beating pulse. Truthfully, he felt terribly sad. He hugged her back just as firmly and listened to her regather herself. He told her how sorry he was. He didn't feel that he had to say anything else; now wasn't the time to ask questions. When her breaths spaced themselves apart and she'd finally relaxed, she walked down towards the river, her legs hopping on the backs of mossy boulders with no hesitation.

The air was still warm, but the sun's brightness had slightly dimmed as it lowered itself in the west. Shadows from the wood grew long, stretching themselves out over the water. The darkness danced and whirled over the torrent; it was the mighty Kennebec, the same river that wound its way through the woods and lined the Libby's blueberry fields, yet Noah had never seen its body from where he was standing now.

As they walked, the river grew wider. The shadows that once painted themselves across the whole surface now barely stretched halfway across. The rapids slowed themselves down until they moved in a lazy current. The trees on the sides had grown taller. More and more rocks gradually appeared on the shore. Not before long, small cliffs began to pop up.

"I think we're getting close," she said.

Maegan's comment startled Noah, causing a delayed rush of blood to his feet—a feeling he normally got when someone would jump from out behind a corner and scare him; he'd been so depersonalized that he'd forgotten the silence that blanketed over the two of them.

"When've you been here?" he asked, attempting to take advantage of the morsel she'd given him to start a conversation.

She searched for an answer. He waited.

"One day last summer," she started, "when Shaun and I were arguing about.... I don't know. Something stupid. I ran up the road and into the woods, the same spot we went in earlier. Anyway, I walked for a while, just going straight. It felt like.... It felt like a hook was latched on my back, pulling me towards something. I knew that something was there, up ahead, so I kept going. I found the hole in the woods and then I found the river. I walked a while and then.... I found that."

Before he could ask, *"Found what?"* he'd already turned his head and seen her arm stretched and pointed straight ahead.

As flat as a book cover and as white as a piece of paper, a sixty-foot cliff stood on the other side of Maegan's index finger. It reminded him of the coast of Cutler he'd once visited, far off in Washington county, where black waves sprayed themselves against weathered rocks. This cliff was peaceful like no other, though; absent of sea salt and the crashing tides, it stood proud and dry. The lethargic current swept past the cliff's foot in ways that didn't challenge its placement. The sun hit its top and glimmered like a halo.

"It's incredible," said Noah.

Maegan gave a teary-eyed smile in his direction.

As the two walked their way down the riverside, the cliff kept getting taller and taller. The closer that they got to it, Noah could see that its face wasn't as clean as it'd looked from farther back. Scars were riddled from its top to its bottom, looking like tiny, jagged cuts etched all over its face. At its base was a sloping rock; it was wide, short, smooth, and sloped its way down until its end just barely dipped in the teal-blue river. After a rainstorm, Noah wouldn't be all that surprised if he could use it as a water slide.

As a precautionary to not slip down its glossy surface, Maegan took off her shoes and worked her way to the top of the rock on her hands and knees, stopping where it finally plateaued for a few feet before meeting the rock wall. Now standing, she spread her fingers open wide in such a way that made Noah think of someone trying to palm a basketball. She placed her hands against the white surface and closed her eyes. Her back slouched slightly, her arms weakened, and her mouth perked into a smile.

"It's warm today."

Noah didn't know if she expected him to do the same thing, nor did he care. He'd walked all this way to see what was in front of him, and maybe he'd imagined it, he surely had, but it felt like his body was gravitating toward the crag. He didn't resist the motion, and after he climbed the slope and reached the wall, he noticed Maegan had started hugging it the best she could; her cheek was squished against the surface, her smile had grown to a wide beam. Noah stretched his hands as wide as humanly possible and touched the white cliff. As he put his palms against its surface, Maegan covered her hand over one of his.

The word *golden* came to him before he could begin to comprehend the feelings that charged through his body. His hands felt warm and smooth, and he could start to feel his lips curl. Every muscle in his body had been loosened; it felt like he'd just come out from a deep massage. His feet stayed locked to the rock beneath him, like a tree almost, with his roots stretching far beneath the flat floor, meandering underneath the water to his back and through the dirt in front of him. He could hear his heartbeat more clearly than he ever had in his entire life. Each beat came with a recognition of him being alive, and safe, and happy. And the visuals! Behind his closed eyelids, different colors and shapes danced their way in front of their black backdrop in the most pleasing ways; visions of abstract trees and bright blue skies, of gradient sunsets, and of many more things that Noah couldn't even wish to decipher.

Upon opening his eyes, he found himself in a similar position to the one he'd seen Maegan in just before his hands had touched the wall: cheek smushed, palms wide. She walked down and sat on the sloped rock below him, hugging her knees and looking out onto the lazy current cross in front of her. Her dark hair draped itself upon her shoulders, with the smallest strands of it glittering with auburn. Noah felt a sudden warmth in his chest that couldn't be anything less than a great affection; the feeling was stronger than any he'd ever felt in his entire life. He went beside her and sat down. He didn't know what to say, though his intuition told him that what had just happened was something to be soaked in without discussion.

"We can talk about Katie now, if you want," Maegan said, again breaking a long and lost period of silence.

"Only if you want to. I don't want to make you sad or

anything."

She smiled, and it was at that moment Noah understood why they'd walked to where they were.

"No, you're very important to me. I want to tell you."

Before he could acknowledge the compliment, she began again.

"Katie told me a while ago, maybe a year or two, that her mom had something wrong with her chest,"

Her voice sounded relaxed, resilient.

"Since then, she'd been getting surgeries pretty often on it. I don't know exactly what was wrong with her. I never asked, anyway—" Her voice trembled, and her eyes flooded with water again. She hugged her knees tight, but she didn't cry.

Noah's mind scrambled; his own death seemed more likely now, even inevitable. The more time he spent on it, the more he convinced himself that he'd be the one who'd be dying next. It was absurd, he thought, that only five or so hours ago Katie was immersed in a soccer game in gym class, unaware of the life altering news that she'd be receiving at any moment. The river kept running and crashed into rocks on the side.

"Do you believe in God?" Noah asked her quietly; the words spilled out of him without an effort to be held back. Maegan took some time to digest the question and return with a fit answer.

"Something like that."

X

KATIE Ross didn't come to school for the next three weeks. The news of her mother's death had echoed around the halls of the school the day after Maegan had told Noah, exponentially spreading until every student in every grade had heard. An obituary was soon put out in the local paper. Donna Ross was thirty-nine. Two weeks after her passing, a celebration of life was held over in Woodrow's Church. Noah initially had responded to the R.S.V.P. as going, though the morning of the event he'd changed his mind. The ultimate decision came during the walk to his car, when he'd stopped to stare at the reflection of himself in the passenger seat window; he'd envisioned Katie's family crying, and Katie herself asking Noah for support. In the days that followed, he tried his best not to think about the culpability of his actions—a pursuit that proved to be a challenge. Time moved on, and twenty-two days after her mother's death, Katie was back in her seat in Mr. McKinley's classroom. Every time Noah looked her way, he couldn't help but feel sick to his stomach with guilt.

It was late April now; the snowbanks had all shrunken to icy sharp black mounds, and some of the dead trees were once again budding with small green pods. It'd rained hard and steady almost every day since Noah had first visited the cliff. His birthday, the fifteenth of May, was fast approaching. Every year, the day felt like a checkpoint, and crossing it meant that the end of school was in sight and the beginning of summer break was closer than ever. This year, however, he wasn't too excited for the annual change.

Noah was laying on Maddy's belly one morning, asking himself questions that he couldn't answer, all of which posed a sharp contrast to the philosophies he had in January and February. *Why is everyone so eager for the year to wrap up?* Back in the winter, he'd wished every morning to open his drapes and magically find it to be June. Even though he told himself that classes didn't matter, that summer was right around the corner, that he'd see everyone again in the fall, he slowly grew more anxious with time. It wasn't the workload that Mack had warned him upwards of ten thousand times that made him worried—far from it, actually. The most daunting realization was a fear that he tried to tuck away: his days of being a kid were numbered, and high school was the final checkpoint in his childhood. Unlike he used to with his birthday, he didn't want to think about crossing it.

"She doesn't want you sitting on her like that," said Mack in passing. Noah didn't care to respond.

He thought about change regularly, often zoned out in the same classes he was fearful of leaving and daydreaming in rooms he wanted to preserve forever. All around the school, he started noticing asymmetries he'd never spotted. Paintings he'd only ever glanced at were crooked, spaces between windows were uneven, and the murals that lined the halls were arranged at slightly different heights.

While Noah spent his days soaking in surrounding mistakes, time acted funny again—April had ended, and May had unobtrusively begun. The rain showers that succeeded Donna Ross's death had subsided; rays of sun shot through Noah's window every morning, waking him up earlier each day while the season neared the solstice. The farm outside of his bedroom window had sprouted with thousands of small bushes, all soaking in something they'd been deprived of for months. None of the blueberries had begun to show, but soon enough little green balls would pop up and resemble the leaf pods which sprouted on the elm tree. Noah's father had been using the warm weather to perform maintenance on the farm; he'd made a to-do list the size of a novel to get the bushes ready for harvest season in July.

Weeks before the good season would arrive, on what happened to be the first Saturday in May, he'd asked Noah to help him man the perimeter. The previous year, the farm had been terrorized by all sorts of animals for food. As a result, a quarter of the harvest was taken away. This year, the Libby's had reinforcements. Noah's father had told him that the traps he bought could crack a bear's bone if stepped into. As for the operation itself, Noah's job was to help place the traps every fifty yards along the sides of the blueberry fields, eventually creating a colossal circle of black jaws.

They started their work earlier than Noah would've liked. Normally, Saturdays were the mornings he got to sleep in (as work was Sunday's problem), so the seven AM wake-up was, simply put, tough. At the sound of his blaring alarm, Noah could've sworn that his mattress was ten times more comfortable than it'd been the day before. After twenty minutes of listening to beeping, his muscles revived, and a very reluctant and tired boy finally started his day. His first order of business was to get changed, so he haphazardly rummaged through his bureau, a process that ended with him putting together an outfit that could've been picked out by Samuel. His pants were stained all over, his socks mismatched, and he had a striped zip up over a striped t-shirt (both with distinctly different sized stripes).

He waddled his way to the middle house, his nose pointed up and taking in the familiar aroma of fried bacon waft from the kitchen through the main hallway. His father had been up for hours already, and that, Noah thought, was *not* hyperbole. Like his eldest son, Patrick Libby would usually be found sleeping in on a Saturday. However, while the stars were still clear, he'd left the farmhouse and driven fifty miles each way to pick up the traps he thought had already been delivered. The seller had threatened to throw them out if they weren't out of his garage by six o'clock.

Upon arriving in the kitchen, Noah found a heaping plate of bacon, along with a gray, sullen looking man that sat directly behind it. His father only drank coffee once in a blue moon, and, despite desperately needing a pick-me-up, it appeared that he had been stubborn and only allowed himself a glass of O.J. Noah's mother had already been up for an hour or two now; she never would set an alarm, yet would always be the first one downstairs each morning. With a flick and a whoosh, she'd start the stovetop and put her oats in with some water. Another pot would heat in the back until it whistled. A few minutes later she brought her oatmeal (now mixed up with one scoop of peanut butter, two of Greek yogurt, a few dashes of cinnamon, blueberries, and gobs of honey) along with her cup of coffee into the living room. Every morning she used the same bowl, wide and gray and shallow, and the same cup, skinny and tan and tall. She was in the same spot now, wrapped up on the couch in a blanket that she folded each night just to unravel again hours later.

Noah's father had hardly spoken to him during the

operation. All he'd say were the same boring instructions each time the two had stopped at a plot. It sounded like he was reading from a script. He'd always been a man of few words, but Noah knew that fatigue was the cause for his present condition. When they'd approached the final five or so plots, his father looked worse than ever. His eyelids had drooped to give off the appearance of a basset hound, and gray stubble appeared to be popping up on his chin. The sun had crawled its way to the top of the sky when Noah and his father had finished up. Over forty traps were now set along the ends of the fields, all opened and waiting to clamp themselves on unsuspecting victims. The father and son both made their way into the house under the clear noon sky. Upon entering, Noah made a beeline for the shower, rushing to take off his cotton t-shirt that chafed the skin around his neck. While he hopped his way up the stairs and to his hallway, he heard the thud of his father fall back into the bedspread he'd longed for.

After Noah's shower and nap, the day had shifted to nighttime. The season was changing fast. Weather was humid. Windows had been cracked. Crickets filled the fields with white noise. Downstairs, Mack had cooked chicken on the skillet and tossed a bowtie pasta salad. At the sound of "Dinner!", Sharon and Samuel were sad to leave 'Fort Libby', a base they'd constructed where the living room couch used to be. His father had just woken up from a six-hour nap. Summer, school ending, high school beginning—it all felt nearer. While he ate, Noah couldn't help but think about the time that was elapsing so quickly. There he sat, both his elbows on the dining room table, looking through great clear window pains and watching the sad sky dim while everyone else discussed their days and shared their plans with one another.

Under instruction to do so, Noah cleared the table of dirty plates and crumpled napkins. Sharon and Samuel had run back to their fort. His father had gone to take his second shower of the day and perhaps go back to bed. The chef was excused of all her duties, and his mother started on the dishes in a kind gesture to help her son out. Noah was putting the forks and knives back into their spots when she turned his way.

"You know, your birthday's coming up."

"Ten days," he replied over the clunking silverware.

"Yes, ten days," she said, pausing. "What could I get for you that would make me the best?"

Noah could see the question coming from a mile away. He still tried to act surprised.

"Oh, I wasn't even thinking about gifts."

"Really?"

"Yeah."

"Mhm? Well, I'll get you nothing."

She turned away, smiling all the while, and started to scrub off scallions and marinade that'd stuck to the plates. Noah hadn't the slightest clue what he wanted, let alone needed. Everything he owned was doing a fine enough job. He brainstormed until she stopped her scrubbing and walked away; he had no idea what she could be thinking.

For what Noah's mother thought, I wish not to say in an explicit manner, and had hoped to follow suit with the structure of the story thus far, as it is cardinal to describe Noah's unfiltered philosophies and curiosities as they are presented. Claire Libby's smile, though, is an exception, as it was a complex expression of nostalgia and maturity—a face one could only produce from looking from the outside in; for she had once been concerned with the very same inconsequential worries that now dominated Noah. As she left the kitchen, a rush of electricity had flowed about her in a way that took her back; for while she was walking to Fort Libby to play with her two youngest, her soul was transported back in time to Bridgton, enveloped in the emotions she had had on a November night when her own mother had interrogated her. Both moments of the past and present, despite them being separated by thirty years, held hands tightly with each other—a pairing which operated on a timeline unknown to clocks and calendars.

XI

TOMORROW was Maegan's birthday, a week and a half before Noah's own. Despite it being so soon, Noah still didn't know what to get her. He racked his brain for ideas in his bedroom while lying above the sheets that topped his mattress. As he thought of potential presents, he tossed a tennis ball up at the ceiling, throwing it just hard enough so it grazed the white paint and fell back down into his outstretched hand. He thought hard, constantly writing and crossing out the ideas he'd bulleted down on a mental note pad. All the things she appreciated were already at her house, hidden behind a broken brick wall in her second story bathroom. *Buy her paint and some brushes?* She surely had enough of each. *Sketch a drawing?* Not a chance. *Clothes?* He looked down at his big toe poking out of his sock and couldn't help but laugh at the thought of him picking out a shirt for

Maegan. The only other interest he could think of was her love for trees; but really, what could he do? He imagined himself slinging a shovel over his shoulder, waltzing into the woods, and returning with a birch in his arms. Any light that lingered after dinner was now gone, and Noah could hardly see the tennis ball before it came back and touched his hand after each throw. He stopped tossing it and subsequently turned onto his side and fell asleep. The clock had only just struck seven.

It was pitch black outside the next time he woke up. All his day-clothes were still on, and his body was still weak from sleepiness; he'd stayed over at Sam's father's house on Friday night and hadn't gotten a wink of sleep. Whether his rouse was caused by a sound or an awkward body position, he didn't know. Despite having to go to the bathroom, he stripped his jeans and t-shirt and crawled under his covers. Maegan's gift, whatever it would turn out to be, was still on his mind. Again, he thought of trees, visualizing the roots and branches she painted on her bedroom walls. He began to drift off again before his bladder caught himself and he got up to go take a pee. With a swing of his legs out over his bed, he reached over with his right arm and switched on his light. An idea shot into his mind in perfect synchronization with the shine of gold that filled his walls. He jumped on the idea so he wouldn't be at a loss in the morning.

After snatching his t-shirt off the floor and making a quick twenty-five second detour to the bathroom, he flipped the latch to the trapdoor above his head. A wooden ladder came down, and as silently as he could step (it must have been past midnight—everything was so quiet), he made his way up the creaking steps. Before he reached the top pegs, he tied the t-shirt he'd grabbed around his ears and over his nose and mouth. The attic was too dark to identify anything, so a tap of the box revealed to Noah that it was just where he'd left it. Blind as a bat, he rummaged the insides at random. To his delight, the bind of an old book caught his index finger. Noah tucked the book into his arms in unison with his eyes glancing up at his surroundings.

The circle window on the far side of the room mirrored the darkness within its walls; the only light came from the moon, a dull presence that dimly illuminated the farm grounds. He gingerly walked his way over to the windowsill, making sure he wouldn't break any stray ornaments and wake his parents up.

The glass was cold to the touch; since sundown, things had cooled down remarkably. Outside, things looked uncommonly still. No wind was in the air, and if the clouds hadn't coasted so slowly under the moonlight, the landscape would look like that of a painting. Everything in sight masked itself in a shade of cool blue. He wondered how he could've forgotten about the remarkable view. The only other time he'd sat there was months earlier, the day he'd discovered a box of misfit possessions.

He sat in his spot and stared out onto his family's land—all of it vast and silent. Noah had a tough time imaging that not a single animal could be out in such a great space of land. The tiny blueberry bushes were paralyzed like cursed stone, the tall trees daring not to sway. It seemed like the clouds also decided to stay stationary for a bit. All was immobile, and all was quiet. Noah could hear his heart beating slowly and steadily.

Not before long, his mind wandered due to both tiredness and boredom. He attempted to think of what he wanted to get for presents when his own birthday came around. He came up blank again and moved on to ponder how he'd wrap up the book he'd be giving to Maegan. *Do you even wrap up books?*

Then, the thought of the deer he'd seen months ago passed his mind. The image hadn't faded. He wondered about all the animals he couldn't see—the ones just beyond the outer rim of the fields. *There's a whole world back there: moving, awake, alive.* The trees were inky; the far line on the horizon that once looked like The Blueridge was now a blotch of blackness, the hills that ebbed away now lost in the clouds.

The painting that once was trapped in amber had awoken. Definite movements down on the field shook the windless and navy night, like ripples in a glassy pool. Like he'd done months earlier, Noah cupped his hands around his eyes, his pinkies pressed against the cool glass wall and his thumbs jammed into his temples. Down below and some eighty yards out, weaving its way amongst the dirt mounds, was the unmistakable outline of a human. Whoever they were, they looked to be the size of a woman or a short man. Their body looked unnaturally skinny, and their legs glided across the field in a peculiar way. The more Noah looked, the more frightened he became. They looked like a ghost. *Maybe they were.*

Despite the figure moving closer to the house, it was impossible for Noah to distinguish any features; the night was much too dark, and they were still hundreds of feet away. In a split second, the thing made an abrupt turn to their right, cutting their way through a vein in the field and towards the trees. It seemed something had caught their attention, and so they walked fast with their back bent low through a canal of dirt. They came to a stop at the edge of the woods. Ten minutes had passed (or so it felt like ten minutes), and the only sounds and movements Noah could discern came from his own chest—his heart pounding as if it was about to pop itself out of his ribcage. Then the thing emerged, accompanied by another. Both were crouched so low that it was impossible to recognize anything about them. All that Noah could see were clumps moving in the darkness. Step by step, they made their way closer to the farmhouse. A group of clouds lazily migrated their way over the sky and blocked the moon, a movement that made the bodies so poorly lit that Noah knew he couldn't risk looking away—it would be impossible to find them again amongst the darkness. He kept his eyes locked and tried his best not to blink. The cluster of clouds soon cleared away and moonlight illuminated the field again Despite the light being so weak, the dim glow revealed the backs of the bodies.

Their spines poked through their backs in a way that reminded Noah of a dragon; their skin was as white and pale as milk; their hair was as long and unkempt as a stray dog's. The one that'd come out from the woods looked like the size of a child. They couldn't be humans; for their aura was damning of something supernatural. The group of clouds moved back over the moon, and Noah lost their bodies. The attic suddenly felt darker and smaller than it ever had. He moved his way across the platform in a hurry, and then made his way down the wooden ladder. He flipped up the trapdoor and ran to his room.

Now in his bed, he laid as silent and as still as the branches outside. He felt like he'd gone mad; for no sounds ever came— not even a pin drop. He kept his ears perked until they drooped down, his eyes wide open until they slowly shut themselves. He'd wished he hadn't stayed up so late at Sam's. Fatigue had bested him.

XII

THE book's cover was moss green, and the black pine tree in its center looked like it was etched into the cover itself, its branches individually sliced out of the hardcover. None of the pages had been creased, and their edges were as sharp as new. The first few pages exceeded all expectations Noah had for it; there was a whole array of tree sketches, accompanied with little blurbs that detailed their respective drawings. He'd focused on a short, stout one with orbs hanging off its branches.

Mangifera indica, commonly known as mango, or mango tree, is a native Indian flowering plant that can now be found in over eighty countries in the world. It is a member of the sumac and poison ivy family Anacardiaceous. The sketch above is a juvenile mango, as most mangoes can grow to be over ninety feet high. Back in the early 18th century....

Underneath the definition of the tree was a drawing of great detail, where each line in the trunk had its own start and finish. All the dashes and crosses worked their way up the bark and out onto long and rigid branches which all sprouted with leaves. It took counting forty of them to decide that there had to be thousands more. Each was drawn with such care, as if every tiny detail was of paramount importance to the whole. He continued flipping through the first five or ten pages before concluding that it was the perfect present to give to Maegan.

The sun had risen hours ago and would soon reach the top of the sky; its beams filtered their way through Noah's window shades and painted streaks on his covers. He was still in his boxers and a way-too-baggy t-shirt, in no immediate hurry to start his Sunday. His legs were crisscrossed over one another in his bed, his elbows jutting into his thigh, his palm holding up his chin, and his fingers flipping through the old pages of a forgotten and beautiful book.

"What were you doing last night?"

The book slipped out of Noah's hands and tumbled onto the floor with a resounding *thump*.

"Don't do that!"

"Do what?"

"Sneak up on me!"

"It's *noon.*"

While she sounded out the closing *n*, Mack's eyes caught the green cover on the floor, the corners of which were now slightly damaged from the fall. Noah picked up the book in a hurry, but quickly realized that his haste to do so had backfired in making his older sister more curious.

"What's that?" she asked.

"What's what?" *Dumb response.*

She paused for a moment; her mouth was slightly ajar.

"You're acting weird lately."

Noah tried to cobble a comeback together in his head, but to no avail. Her eyes were still locked on the book that was poorly hidden in Noah's arms.

"Well, anyway," she said while her eyes scanned every corner of her brother's bedroom, "I heard you last night. I don't know what time it was, maybe past two, but when I got up to go to the bathroom, I heard you shut something and run around."

Noah wondered if he ought to tell her what he'd seen. Prior to his sister's appearance, he'd convinced himself that it'd all been an illusion. *But what if it hadn't....*

"Well?"

"Well, what?" he asked absentmindedly.

"Noah! What were you doing last night? And what is that book?"

"Oh."

After struggling to create a lie good enough to fool her, he resigned to telling Mack the truth.

"Well, I went up to the attic to get this book," he said, grudgingly tossing the hardcover on the bunched up covers at his feet, "and I shut the hatch and ran because I was scared."

"What?"

"I shut the hatch and ran becau—"

"I know, I know! But *why?*" she asked with exasperation in her voice.

"Can you please not laugh at me if I tell you?"

"You're being a baby."

Noah looked away.

"I won't laugh," she said desperately.

"Mhm."

"I won't! Just tell me!"

It was difficult to ignore the voices inside his head that told him he shouldn't out of spite. However, Noah knew he had to tell someone what he'd seen.

"You know the small circle window up in the attic?" he asked.

"Yeah, why?" she replied with an air of curiosity and satisfaction in her voice.

"Well, I was looking out of it, and everything was still...."

After going over every painstaking detail and visual description of his story (thrice), a silence fell between the two of them. Noah could tell Mack was troubled by what she'd heard.

"Noah, ghosts aren't real."

"They weren't people, remember? I said—"

"Ghosts *aren't* real," she said again, this time sounding out each syllable as if she was speaking to a preschooler.

"I know what I saw."

Noah couldn't tell if Mack had even heard his reply.

"Regardless of what you thought you saw, I'm telling Dad and Mom. I think someone was trying to rob us."

Noah decided he couldn't stop her from telling them. He let out a sigh, closed his eyes, and fell back into his pillows. Against the black backdrop of his close eyelids, he conjured up what he'd seen hours before. It wasn't difficult to imagine their milky and tot skin against their hard bones; their bodies were as clear now as they'd been the night before.

"I never pegged you for being much of an arborist, you know," muttered Mack.

"Hey!"

She pulled back the book from Noah's outstretched hands and close to her chest.

"Give it!"

"Why are you freaking out? It's a book about trees. Why is it such a big deal when I look at it? Seriously?"

And so, they sat—Mack flipping through the pages, and Noah counting the seconds until she closed the covers. It felt like an eternity.

"Okay! I'm done now," she said as she tossed the book up in the air and into Noah's lap.

"Is everything up to your standards?"

"Yes, yes, but I do have one question."

Although Noah had both his hands held out, his sister kept the book gripped in her own.

"What does 'From N to M' mean exactly?" asked Mack. She cracked a smile and pointed, her finger underlying the addition Noah had written on the inside cover earlier that morning. He reached over and snagged the book before Mack could pull it back. She got up, smiling all the while, and made her way out into the hallway.

"You know," she started from out in the hall, "you're not as bad of a boyfriend as I thought you were, No'."

He sat slack jawed, the book still clutched in his arms, listening to his older sister whistle her way down the stairs. It took him a bit, but he couldn't help but smile back.

* * *

"I swear, it *really* is! It couldn't be any better—it couldn't!"

Maegan sat crisscrossed while she leafed through the crisp cream pages. By her side was a red ribbon that Sharon had offered to wrap around the book; it was added after Mack had unsurprisingly spread the news of Noah's gift to the entire family. Poor Sharon felt awful upon Noah's reaction to her knowing, and, sincerely as ever, had offered the accent as a peace offering. Samuel just laughed.

Maegan and Noah were perched at the top of the highest hill of the neighboring conservatory, far enough out where Noah's home appeared as just a red speck against a powder blue sky. The sun had lowered itself, and Maegan and Noah's bodies now generated long dark silhouettes against the new green grass. Maegan had been making remarks about the brilliance of the present every few minutes for the last hour. Noah had been lying on his back and staring at wispy clouds slowly disperse into the darkening backdrop. Time had slowed down for the first time in forever.

"May is by far the most pleasant month of the year," said Maegan; she was pulling stems of grass from the ground and making a pile in her lap. Noah nodded; he could feel his lips curl into a smile that was far from forced. Maegan had noticed him do so, and the look was apparently contagious. *May is, by far, the most pleasant month of the year.*

"My gift for you isn't as good," she said quietly out into the air. "I'm sorry."

"You already got a gift for me?"

"Well yeah! You had this gift ready for me, didn't you?"

Noah spun his head at her with wide eyes and raised

eyebrows.

"What? Why are you looking at me like that?" she asked.

A second later, they both laughed and fell back onto the carpet of grass. The small wisps had all separated into even smaller ones. The sun was falling faster. The two of them stared at the sky, pointing at different spots that they found to be pretty. They did this by chunking out bits and bobs of the environment, constructing puzzle pieces that held their own tones and pallets—a method that allowed them to frame the whole scene and appreciate the tiny little nuances of it all. Maegan was moved by a chemtrail left by a plane. Noah couldn't get enough of the electric blue painted above his eyes. A time came when they got up and headed down the hill en route to Shelley Avenue. When they'd done so, neither of them had asked the other if they were ready to go; it was one of those special moments when two stand together underneath an umbrella.

Crickets sounded off behind the white fence to the right of their steps, and a train blew its tall horn somewhere far, far away. Noah loved the sound of a train whistle blowing. It calmed him. Someone, a someone who he'd never know, nor would ever know of him, was out traveling and working while he could lie down and be still, especially when he went to bed, able to soak in the world around him and bask in its solace. The structure of everything was confusing but beautiful; he couldn't contextualize it, but he knew that he liked the way things worked and was at peace with not knowing who the conductor was. He was just another person—a cog in a machine that spins and clicks and motors on each day and each night. He was too oblivious to see the contradiction his daydreams had to his fear of aging.

Noah's thoughts carried him onto the cracked pavement. The walk up the hill and to the farmhouse felt shorter than it'd ever felt for him. He stepped off the white line and onto the gravel driveway.

"Thank you, again," said Maegan, her hands crossed in front of her polka dotted skirt.

"Yeah—you're welcome. Well, goodnight I guess."

Before he could move a muscle, she'd already leaned in and kissed his cheek. In an instant, his entire head felt on fire and his heart began to beat at ten beats per second. He didn't know what to say.

"Oh."

Maegan let out a snort and turned to finish the walk back to her house. The sky was now purple, and everything seemed much crisper than it'd been only a minute ago. Once his legs finally had feeling in them again, he turned and walked his way toward his lit kitchen. He'd looped what had happened in his head several times before he reached the mudroom steps and stood on the highest one. He could see Samuel next to the island in the kitchen; he was explaining something to his mother with overexaggerated hand movements, while she sat opposite of him on a stool and nodded. Noah couldn't read his lips through the glass.

XIII

MAY fifteenth, 2001, held sunshine which bested that of the day when Noah had first visited the white cliff. By the time he'd gotten up, Maddy had already ran around the field and tired herself out. Birds sang their spring songs, and a woodpecker worked on the branch of a tree hidden in the green work. Percy was either hunting around his barn or stalking vowels in the shallows of the forest.

Noah had woken up earlier than normal. That morning, there would be no rush to find his clothes tucked about in his drawers, no hearing his mother yell up to his floor about how late he was going to be, and no bedhead. Things would be different. He'd woken up thirty minutes earlier than his typical morning and spent the first fifteen sitting on his bed with his back against his wall. He stared outside, taking in the sounds of the birds and the cloudless sky. His window had been open the entire night before, and a soft morning breeze had found its way into his bedroom. The clothes he'd planned to wear were laid out on the chair opposite of where he sat. He pulled on his green striped t-shirt and navy shorts and turned to his mirror; after several minutes of adjusting his light brown hair he gave up on making it any neater.

Sharon ran around the outside of the house like it was a big planet, and she was a tiny satellite stuck in its pull. Every time she looped the house, she ran her hands to touch a garden, bending down and stretching her arm out so just the tips of her fingers would graze petals. The garden was right near where the white wicker wrap-around porch stepped down, behind the mudroom and near the back of the middle house. The garden wasn't Noah's father's, nor his mother's, nor Samuel's, nor Mack's, nor his own—it all belonged to Sharon. A batch of tulips (now dead) began the lineup of purple lupins and mulch soon to sprout with sunflowers. On the weekends, she normally would sit outside and draw them in a tattered green journal she'd gotten from her mother for Christmas. It was May, and the journal's pages were almost all the way full. Half the pages alone ranged the past month—almost all brief sketches of tulips with splotches of watercolors done in post. School being soon made it impossible for her to get a sketch in, so she resorted to circling her muses instead. She was rather silent about her documentation; for it wasn't made for anyone else but herself (and didn't need to be to survive). Her consideration was enough, as the abstractions she'd created had let her meditate on something that made her genuinely happy. If anyone else saw, that'd be okay, too. Her adaptations weren't necessarily 'good' by any technical standards (whatever that means), but they were fixed to Sharon—bound to her imagination so strongly that they carried souls linked to their owners. Sharon's drawings were like lightning in a bottle: futile and universal, unbiased towards raw emotions, and resisting any potential sway from those who are older. Documenting that is the closest thing to magic.

May fifteenth was without question one of Noah's favorite days, yet every year it felt like his mother was more excited about his birthday than he was himself. This year she'd put Mack in charge of making a heaping pile of pancakes while she wrapped presents up in her bedroom. His father was excused from all birthday jobs, as he'd been busy the past few days setting up a security system for both the front and mudroom doors. Tonight, his mother would be making his favorite Shepherd's Pie and a strawberry rhubarb crisp. She'd adopted the recipes as her own, though they both belonged to Mrs. Murphy. Sam and Warren had come over for dinner the past two years and had already agreed to come for a third straight time. Noah thought about his mother's underappreciated goodwill while he squeezed his way past Samuel and into the brightly lit kitchen.

After he wolfed down four piping hot chocolate chip pancakes, Noah grabbed his school bag and rose from his stool. Before he could reach the mudroom, Sharon roared into the kitchen like an October hurricane, wiping sweat off her brow and huffing loudly. She swung open the door of the cabinet closest to the sink and immediately rummaged through its rows to grab the biggest cup she could find.

"Wash your hands," Mack observed, barely glancing at her little sister to keep eyes on the griddle.

Out of his house now, at the top of the three short and steep entry steps of his school bus, Noah was met with a loud and excited buzz of several conversations that came from his fellow schoolmates—a worthy reaction to the first leg of a special day at Thredsum Middle School. Two weeks out of the school year (once in the fall and once in the spring), parent-teacher conferences are held to give an update on students' performances. Wednesdays, Thursdays, and Fridays are when most parents sign up for a time to meet, and so, to prepare for the influx of appointments, the school always chose to cut those days in half. The fifteenth fell on a Wednesday, the first of the three days in which Noah would be dismissed at 11:30 sharp.

As he walked from row to row, the excitement stayed true. The buzzing made it impossible to pick up even half of the conversations, yet Noah could make out some of the passing chatter on his way to the back of the bus. Closer to the steps he'd just climbed up from, he caught a girl mentioning a secret swimming hole she'd found in the river. Somewhere in the middle of the bus, he heard a high-pitched voice mention how a certain group was planning on biking over to their house for lunch. Now near the back, he made out the sound of a boy with a deep voice boasting about the three cans of beers he'd stolen from his older brother and stashed into his backpack. Everybody had their own plans ready for what they'd be doing the second the bell boomed. Noah smiled at the thought of his own plan when that time came.

The back left seat was occupied by a regular whose hair had flecks of shining auburn and whose shirt had thirty different small frogs screened on. Her smile met the energy of the babbling that surrounded them.

"You're fourteen!" shrieked Maegan.

"Why do you sound so surprised?"

"I'm not, really—I just got used to being older than you."

To the right of Maegan was a small box wrapped in rainbow striped paper with a small white bow on its top.

"Well, here it is," she said, pushing the small box into Noah's hands as he sat himself down onto the hard gray seat. His fingers rotated it around to see every corner.

"Open it!"

Noah was meticulous in how he did so; the paper she'd used to wrap with was so clean and pretty he would've felt bad if he tore it in front of her.

"I had to change what I was going to give you after you got me the book, you know—this one's more, well, I don't know, you'll see."

She tried pausing for a moment while Noah unstrapped the tape. It didn't take long for her patience to break.

"Just open it!"

"I'm getting there!"

Inside the wrapping was a black box that looked big enough to hold a watch. A horizontal seam crossed the middle and marked its opening. The mouth had a slight magnetic pull that held its doors shut. He pulled open the mouth and swung the top half of the box up and away from him. Inside the box was a small and wooden oval with metal on its sides; it looked remarkably smooth and was undoubtedly brand new. Noah picked it up and placed it flat in the palm of his hand. He knew exactly what it was—his father had one that looked just like it. He pulled at the notches in the metal, and within seconds the wooden oval had grown ten arms—one serrated like a knife, and another thin and pointy in the slim outline of tweezers.

"Woah," whispered Noah. "This is sweet."

"It's a Swiss Army Knife!"

"I know, I know. I love it," he said in between laughs.

Maegan beamed and simultaneously let out an audible breath of relief. She turned her shoulder and stared out the window at the homes and yards they whizzed past. Noah kept his eyes on his gift, smiling.

* * *

11:29 came mighty fast. Not only were the classes shorter, but they were also substantially easier, as all of Noah's teachers had the preconception that the class period was much too short to get any work done. Mrs. Hannings, however, looked as if she'd just remembered that a scheduled afternoon of non-stop meetings was ahead of her. Above her desk, the small red hand of her clock slid its way past the six, then the seven, then the eight. Every two or three seconds she cocked her head back at it, looking each time as if the hands were going to spin counterclockwise and she'd have more time to prepare her notes. At the beginning of the period, she hastily told Noah's class to open their notebooks to a certain chapter and relate it to their final project. She was too preoccupied to notice no one had done so.

The school bell blared its way through the hallways, smothering a *"Damn!"* and generating a wave of squeaking shoes and chattering voices. To avoid the rush, Noah chose to be the last to leave the room. Once he'd finally made his way out into the hallway and through the great big front doors, he was met with an overwhelming and beautiful scene. In front, behind, and beside him, everyone rushed into the eighty-degree May air; some made beelines to unlock their bikes from the racks, some grouped up outside the big front doors and talked plans, some ran around the school to the soccer fields. Katie Ross and Georgia Winnings were laughing about something as they walked their way near a larger group of girls; it was the first time Noah had seen Katie laugh in a long while.

Noah made his way past a gathering crowd and met Sam and Warren next to the statue of Augustus Rulch's brilliantly shining bronze head. Sam wore a dark blue t-shirt along with baggy black shorts that were threatening to come down every time he took a few steps. Warren sported a bright red basketball jersey with the head of the Thredsum Tiger on its front. The latter looked sullen as ever. Drew Carlin had broken up with him two weeks prior.

"I know she's not happy," Warren shot out to Noah while spinning his head away from a group of girls. "She can't be—I mean, look at her."

Noah turned to where Warren had been staring and found Drew in the crowd of people he'd just passed to get to the statue. She was in the middle of them, smiling and laughing, oblivious to anybody who might (on the off chance) be glaring in her direction.

"Yeah man, you're better than her," said Sam halfheartedly as he looked over a sea of sixth graders move past them.

"Yeah, you are," added Noah, trying to be sincere.

"Whatever."

"River?" Sam asked. The other two almost couldn't hear the question over the clunking sounds coming from him loosening a drawstring bag. "I've got Yoo-hoo—'bout six bottles' worth."

Warren nodded slowly, keeping both his eyes locked on Drew. Noah coughed to suppress a laugh and nodded as well. After a few moments, Warren regathered himself and stood up to join Sam and Noah as they walked towards the road.

XIV

IT took roughly fifteen minutes of walking along the sides of busy roads to reach a line of cars, all which were parked in a grassy stretch that sat flat in between the pavement and dark evergreens. As he passed them, Noah noticed that every back windshield had a Thredsum High School Parking Pass stuck to its glass. After ten or so cars, Sam made a right and walked past a tiny brown sign with a carved arrow pointed to the heart of the woods. Warren and Noah followed Sam's footsteps as they transitioned from soft grass to hard roots and tough dirt. When Noah stepped onto the trail, the sudden coolness made him notice his shirt had gotten soaked with sweat. The radiant sunshine no longer burned his neck, but rather bounced off tree trunks and illuminated leaves until it lit up the dark forest floor like a lime green mosaic. Even with such dense woods, the sunlight found its way through every opening; everything in sight had turned remarkably crisp, displayed in an assortment of browns, greens, and golds.

As they made their way single file through the tight trail, they covered an assortment of extensive conversations. Warren had kicked off their trek by arguing about the importance of good grades, or lack thereof, for college acceptance—a stance both Sam and Noah fully supported. The subject transitioned to Noah discussing how stressed Mack always is, which led to Warren discussing how attractive Mack is, which then promptly led to Noah telling him to shut up, which then was interrupted with Sam swearing loudly over of a toe he'd stubbed on a root. After a long back and forth between Warren and Noah concerning what was acceptable to say about one's siblings, their attention had shifted, and the argument was abandoned.

Noah guessed there had to be at least twenty people at the spot already. With every step over twisted roots and every turn around a mossy boulder, the clamor grew and grew. Eventually, the three passed the welcome sign (an oak tree with a smiley face carved in its bark) and stepped out onto a slanted rock that stood above the rushing river. Down and to Noah's right was the swimming hole. As expected, two dozen high-schoolers were already there, blasting music on a boombox and splashing around in the water like there was no tomorrow. A few were drinking beer, and almost all of them swore vehemently. A ten-foot waterfall leveled itself out into the calm and deep pool they were stationed in. Everyone in their party had grouped to one side of the swimming hole and faced in the waterfall's direction, cheering on a select few doing flips and twists off the rocks. Before Noah could turn back into the woods, Warren had already made his move and walked down the slant and towards the semicircle of high-schoolers. Noah followed behind Sam, who trailed Warren closely down the rock face. The closer he got, the more the butterflies in Noah's stomach fluttered. Despite them seeming dense and obnoxious, he unquestionably felt grossly intimidated by them.

As if a prayer had been miraculously and immediately answered, the semicircle of teenagers climbed out of the pool and started putting their t-shirts and shoes back on. By the time Warren had reached the base of the pool, some high-schoolers had already started their walk back towards the smiley face. The group of boys who'd just jumped off the rock wall climbed their way out of the pool and found their clothes. One of them (with a fully grown beard) put his arm around a girl that looked like Shauna, just a couple years older.

The other two boys sauntered their way over to Warren; they were both tall and shaggy and were whispering to each other between giggles. One had a patchy mustache, and the other had disgustingly hairy sideburns. They looked to Noah like trouble. One of them laughed and stuck their hand out to Warren to shake, but before he could decide on whether or not he wanted to return the favor, the boy's hand had lowered; his attention had fully shifted to the clinking and clunking happening behind Warren. In what Noah deemed an inexcusably embarrassing move, Sam had decided that now was the best time to take out the six Yoo-hoos he'd brought along. A second of silence was followed by an explosion of cackling from the two boys.

"Sam, put 'em away!" whispered Warren.

"What? Why?"

"Just do it!"

"No, I'm good."

Warren stammered and kept trying to convince Sam otherwise, but Noah knew it was of no use. As kindhearted as he was, Sam was one of the most stubborn people he knew. After the boys' laughter died down, they stepped towards where Sam sat.

"Can I have one?" asked the boy with the mustache, holding out one hand and clenching the other to stop himself from bursting out in laughter.

"Yeah, why not?" answered Sam as nonchalantly as possible.

The boy's fist loosened up.

"Thanks boss," he replied in a more sober voice.

"Here's one for your buddy too," continued Sam, flipping the bottle in his hand and coolly catching it by its neck. The boy with the mustache shifted his eyes back to the boy with the hairy sideburns, who shrugged as if to say: '*I have no clue what's going on right now*'.

"Alright, well, thanks."

And then the two boys walked away, looking equally confused and cheery that they'd somehow each ended up with a bottle of chocolate milk. Noah sat down and started unlacing his sneakers and taking off his socks. Warren did the same. The last of the high-schoolers (being the girl who looked like Shauna, the boy with the beard, and the two boys that Sam just confronted) all left their spot. As he walked past Sam, the boy with the hairy sideburns stopped and swung a duffle off his back and onto the ground. After rummaging through some things, he pulled out a twelve pack of beer and tossed it in Sam's lap.

"Thanks for the Yoo-hoo, boss man."

And then he jogged away, hopping up the rock and back into the middle of the group. For Noah, it was one of those moments that made him feel like he was living in a Hollywood movie. He looked from Sam to Warren, then from Warren to Sam. With a confused smile, Sam shrugged, reached down, pulled a can, and popped it open.

XV

"YOU said *oh?*"

Noah waited until Warren and Sam stopped their howling, which took a couple minutes and some change.

"Mhm."

"But," choked Sam through a wave of giggles, "why?"

"What would you say then?" asked Noah. His eyes were fixed on Warren's Vans as they stepped over roots and rocks.

They roared again.

"No—I wanna know, what would you say?"

"Not *oh*," said Warren.

"Whatever."

Noah knew he couldn't win this one. He was much too disoriented to think of a logical response to win an argument, and so it wasn't long before he'd forgotten about the conversation entirely and moved on. They were walking back to the road, now on the trail where treetops swayed above them in the wind. Sam was humming a song, but maybe Noah was just imagining that. He could feel the water drip from his shorts down onto his feet. The shirt he'd flung over his shoulder kept sliding off. His perception of time was poor. He kept smacking his lips together and swallowed his spit to try and get the taste of bread out of his mouth. It didn't work.

"Ow!" yelled Sam from behind Noah's head. He'd bumped into the same root that he accidentally kicked earlier. Noah and Warren stopped and waited for Sam to run out of cusses before resuming their trip back to the road. Noah looked about the woods while his feet drifted behind Warren's. He reached into his pocket to feel cold metal touched his fingertips; it made him think of Maegan. When he shifted his eyes back towards Warren, he'd noticed that they were only a few yards away from the wooden sign with the carved arrow. The road was right ahead of him. He'd never drank alcohol before (only wine on Christmas the year before, but according to Sam, that didn't count) let alone been drunk.

"Time moves funny, right?" Noah asked the others. Warren looked back and nodded with a grin. Sam was still humming some song.

Everything turned white once they stepped out on the road; the sun was ridiculously bright compared to the green tints they'd just walked beneath. After some time, maybe a minute, maybe a few (Noah didn't know), he could finally adjust to the lighting. The road ahead stretched for a mile before it curved left and out of sight. Water vapors above the pavement were distorting the backdrop of trees that sat behind the bend. Noah just wanted to sit down. The only thing that kept him going was the thought of the cold bottle of water he was walking towards. Warren had the same idea; he'd been bouncing a tennis ball he'd found lying alone on the side of the road and spouting out snack and drink orders he had in mind. He just kept talking; it seemed like he wasn't necessarily looking for anybody to respond, more just thinking out loud.

When the boys reached the bend, they stopped to step around a spread of a thousand tiny pieces of broken glass. No one had shoes on, so they took their time. The rest of the pieces of the bottles scattered the neighboring grass, their yellow logos pointed up at the blue sky and the droplets of chocolate milk pooling in unbroken corners.

Noah's shorts and shirt had dried by the time they'd reached the country store; it was at a cost, though, as he could already feel his back and neck heat up. If he hadn't been burnt yet, he'd be surprised. He threw on his green striped t-shirt before finding refuge under the store's awning. A bell sounded when Warren swung open the glass front door. The insides of the store were nice and cool, along with being completely absent from anyone besides the old man that sat behind the counter, writing something down in a journal he balanced on his left thigh. A radio on a shelf behind him hummed with static. He looked up at the boys, to which Noah responded with a nod, and to which the man responded with a small smile and a grunt. After acknowledging the trio, he looked back down at his journal and continued to write. His face was covered in ripples of wrinkles, his eyelids drooped like a dog's, his ears big and floppy, his head topped with strands of thin white hair.

Noah went to the far side of the store and opened the double-door refrigerator to pick out what kind of water he wanted to get. Sam and Warren had migrated to the back of an aisle to get an assortment of chips and candy. When they met back up in front of the counter, Warren had three bags of Utz balanced in between his arms and Sam had gotten a whole array of neon candies. Warren went to pay first. After he'd given the old man a crumpled five-dollar bill, Sam made his way to the wooden tabletop. In the five feet he moved to get there, he managed to drop all six (Noah had the chance to count) of his bags of candy onto the ground before knocking over a tiny kiosk of lollipops.

"Sorry, Sir," Sam mumbled as he got on all fours to pick up his bags and the fallen stand. The old man grunted a similar grunt to the one he'd given Noah upon their entrance, except this time with no smile. While the old man waited for Sam to fish out quarters from a string bag, he placed his journal down on the side of the countertop. He must've not noticed that he'd left his pen inside its pages; for when he put it down, it opened immediately to the page he'd left off on. The corners of the pages fluttered against an artificial breeze from a nearby fan. The book was angled in such a way that Noah could nose in and make out some of the words the old man had written. The top right of the page was marked *Easter '78*, and the top left *p. 299*. Despite being so old, his penmanship was smooth and sharp. Even with the neatness of the entries, Noah was too far away to read everything line by line. He could only find a few words at random; the capitalized ones were the easiest to see. With that being said, it wasn't hard to spot *Deb*. Whoever she was, the old man had written about her almost every single line. The fluttering from the fan had caught the bottom left corner of the page with enough force to flip it over, revealing two more pages of entries. *Lake Sunapee, '88,* was marked in its top left corner, and *Deb* was being penned with a similar frequency. Once Sam had put the last of his quarters on the wooden tabletop, the old man scooped them up with his left hand while his right recovered his open journal. He threw the coins in his register and tossed the book into an open space next to the radio.

Noah's eyes met those of the old man when it came time for him to pay. He'd never noticed it during the countless number of times he'd seen them in the summer seasons, nor when he'd walked under the sounding bell only five minutes ago, but the man behind the counter, someone whom Noah only ever knew as 'Sir', looked to be the loneliest person in the universe. His eyelids drooped lower than they'd ever before, and his posture was lazy, and his hands were all worn, and his eyes were absent of wonder. He stuck out his scarred palm and Noah put his dollar in its center. The door rang and Noah turned to follow his friends out to the store's porch. The man had sat back down with his book and opened it to where he'd left off.

*　*　*

The alcohol wore off Noah as the dinner table got set up. In the room over, Sam, Warren, and himself all sat on the living room rug in anticipation of eating until their stomachs would pop. Maddy was in the corner, gnawing on the tennis ball Warren had picked up earlier. Sunlight still shone through the single window, and when the three boys eventually got the call to come to the table, the sky had changed into a withered blue.

Noah began his family's nightly prayer with being thankful for the gifts he'd already received and closed with a wish that his headache would go away. Sam and Warren both thanked Noah's mother for the meal and made similar wishes to Noah's. After Sharon finished her remarks, which lasted two minutes too long, they dug in.

Noah had never eaten something as fast as he did his plate of Shepherd's Pie and gravy. Although he recognized he was being a pig, he didn't care; the difference in how he felt before and after eating was remarkable. With every bite of buttery mashed potatoes, the ache in his forehead subsided; and with every spoonful of warm minced meat, his alertness gradually came back to him. By his last bite, Noah noticed that Sam's and Warren's plates were both empty as well. Seconds came, then did thirds; it was only a matter of time before Noah's mother had to cut them off. His father was amused by it all.

By the time Noah had surrendered the challenge of finishing his crisp, he felt sober again (or at least he thought he did). He still felt tired, even more so now, and just wanted to lie down. Yes, he felt more aware and coordinated than he had before eating, but fatigue swept over him fast. Below him, Maddy breathed loudly and steadily. His father's foot tapped the ground every second or two. The candles on the table burned dimly. The sky outside had gone black. And then he was drifting.... and although he could still hear voices, he couldn't make out words; all he could gather were tones and pitches with the occasional scratch of a fork across a plate.

The sound of a glass crashing against the ground brought him back to reality. Directly across the table, Sharon had tears in her eyes and was frozen in her seat. Everybody cleared the table while Noah's mother and father helped pick up the pieces of what formerly was a mason jar.

Later, in the living room, Warren and Sam both gave Noah an envelope. He thanked them both but closed by letting them know he was much too tired to open them right now. With a collective yawn, they both agreed. Only some seconds later a car honked, and they made their way towards the mud room.

After a five-minute catnap on the L-shaped couch, Noah's family joined him in the living room and came bearing gifts. He forced himself to wave off the thought of his bed several times. Although difficult, he reminded himself that if he gave a gift to someone, he wouldn't have appreciated a yawn in return. With a great effort, he lifted himself up onto the end of the couch and put a smile on. After unpacking a variety of new clothes and a tall steel water bottle, Noah's mother handed him what appeared to be the last present of the night. The way she'd wrapped it reminded him of the gift he'd opened earlier that morning, and so he took his time in unfolding the corners of paper and prying off the scotch tape that held it down. When he finished, he slid the paper down to the rug below him and uncovered a matt blue cover of a nameless square book he'd never seen before; it was noticeably thin in width and felt worn by time. Upon his mother's nudge, he opened it. Inside the canvas covers were a series of laminated pages that contained an array of photos, all of which were somewhat faded in their color. Noah instantly recognized a younger version of his mother; for she looked just like Mack and was in almost all the prints. In most of the photos, she was with another girl with much shorter hair and a boy with glasses. The backdrops covered brick walls, gas stations, booths of a diner Noah had never been in, and a field somewhere he'd never walked. In almost all of them, she wore a scarlet sweater and the faintest of smiles. The book was far and away the best gift he'd ever been given.

* * *

Noah was already swaddled in covers before he remembered he hadn't yet brushed his teeth, and by the time the thought crossed his mind he couldn't have cared less. Through his opened window, Noah listened to the summer songs of crickets chirping, and occasionally could hear the faint rush of a car on Shelley Avenue. He was slumped on his side in such a comfortable way that he imagined he couldn't move a muscle if he tried. With closed eyes, he recapped the long day and the great gifts he'd been given. He thought of the moment he'd opened the small black magnetic box. He thought of the groups of his classmates that circled themselves outside of the school. He thought of all the steps that he'd walked, trying to remember the scenes of the lime green forest and the humidity that lined the long road he'd been on. With a vivid imagination, he envisioned the high school boys throwing their bottles of chocolate milk out of the window of a speeding car. And then he thought of the old man, all alone in the store, while his fans waved their metal hands and his coffee machine dripped down into a waiting pot. He thought of the look he had in his eyes, and the stories that he'd hidden in a book on his shelf.

Noah was interrupted before he could immerse himself into any more of his thoughts. Far outside his open window, a faint scream dully cut itself through the soft songs of insects. His eyes opened wide, but his body stayed still on its side. He listened closely. After minutes of hearing only the wind, his mind wandered off to theorize who'd screamed and why. It sounded far off, hundreds of yards away. *But why? Why would someone be in the field? Was it the ghosts? Can ghosts even scream?*

He looked out the window, and even with his eyes being fully adjusted to the darkness, he had a hard time seeing anything move. The Earth was hard, and her nature was unforgiving. Night had fallen long ago, and dawn was still a long way away. The wind whipped the tops of oaks that looked like skeletons, sounding identical to a torrent of water—rushing, rushing, rushing.

After minutes of contemplating what had happened, Noah was decently sure that he'd imagined it all. *If someone really did scream, they'd keep screaming, or whimpering at the least.* Despite recognizing the ridiculousness of the hypothetical, his mind traveled to a dark and restless place. Oddly enough, the sound he'd heard had made him think of his mother. He loved her more than anything; for she was the most gracious and caring person in his life. One day, though, Noah thought with open eyes and locked hands, she would be gone forever—just like Katie's mother. The last hour of his birthday was spent grappling with the inevitability of death, chewing over various ways in which he could prevent the reaper from ever paying a visit to his family. The concept frustrated him, and so he eventually let himself drift off and back into the memories of the day that'd just passed.

XVI

NOAH didn't know why he was forbidden to ask questions; it all seemed a little much. Typically, the walk from his house to hers felt like nothing, but now the weather made it feel like it was ten miles long. All along the winding road, wind whipped its way straight into his chest and face, occasionally knocking him back and constantly causing his eyes to tear up. The gusts were accompanied by cold air and overcast skies. The fact that his birthday was only four days ago seemed silly. May now felt like March, and he was alone to feel it all—the stubborn wind crashing onto his flannel, the rain spitting in black slashes on the pavement.

After he reached the top of the last hill, he thought back to what Maegan had told him over the phone the night before. Shauna had to use the line after her, so everything she said was all in a rush. In short, Noah had to take everything he'd put into Emmy's Hollow out by tomorrow evening. Maegan's mother had caught her putting some stuff away, and now planned to use the spot as an extra space for storage (funny enough). She closed by telling him that no one would be home during the whole day tomorrow and shared the spot where she'd hidden her spare house key. That was it. The call lasted two minutes, tops.

It was only two days before the phone call in which they'd been sitting together on her bathroom floor; Maegan's back had been resting on the bathtub, and Noah's own laid against the polka dotted wallpaper beneath the lone window. A Roald Dahl inspired conversation about the homes that mice made within walls evolved into one involving a tunnel system that weaved through the woods and fields that neighbored Shelley Avenue. In giving long and vivid descriptions, Noah and Maegan constructed a whole winter wonderland fantasy, where feet of packed down snow covered all of Thredsum. In accordance to how they imagined it, it was impossible for anyone to leave their homes; roads blended into the fields beside them, and shovels that were left outside only had their handles showing. Starting in their respective backyards, they told each other that they'd both dig in the direction of the others' home until their paths connected exactly in the midpoint. Along with their headlamps, Maegan had added that she'd be using a blowtorch to melt her tunnel, while Noah insisted on using a drill the size of his head.

Their script told that the snowstorm would last ten days and ten nights before any of it'd melted or was plowed away. Each day they'd travel three times—switching on and off which house they'd be eating breakfast, lunch, and dinner at. Both exits from the tunnel were brightly identified with the addition of white Christmas lights that lined the last fifty feet of the trail, connected to generators with oodles of extension cords.

When Noah had eventually reached Maegan's house, the spits of rain grew, now balling themselves into sizable drops. The first scan of the front yard was successful; all the way to the far left of the garden was a big white rock with black spots splattered on its front. Underneath the rock and on top of a layer of mulch was the house key Maegan had entrusted him with.

He made his way up the stairs and stopped at the welcome mat in front of the glass-enclosed porch. With a spin and a click, the door unlatched itself and creaked open. Inside, he climbed the second set of steps to the main door. He opened it and walked into a dark and abandoned house. In his peripherals, he saw a tail scurry itself around a corner and out of sight. All was silent besides the ticking of a clock balanced on the busy shelf ahead of him. Everything around him was blanketed in a collection of blues, greens, and grays; it was odd for him to see such a commonly lively space as empty and silent as it was now.

To his left was the window he'd stared out of months before. Outside, instead of a flat yard of snow, was a garden in preparation of its annual flourish, still some time away from growing a forest of sunflowers. The path had been cleared and little flowers around it popped.

When he reached the top of the narrow staircase, Noah saw the same tail vanish from the hallway and into Maegan's mother's bedroom. He could just barely hear the clock ticking now. Everything else was quiet. Ahead of him, the bathroom door was wide open, and the sink was dripping slightly. He didn't have to shine a light on the wall to find the small X's Maegan had drawn; he'd visited enough times to know exactly where they were. After he pulled each brick out and placed them on the toilet beside him, he reached into the pocket of his zip up and took out a flashlight.

The space that'd once held just a chunk of white rock had grown to foster hundreds of items. So many things were in there—from post-it notes to skipping stones, from baseball cards to rusty keys, almost all found by Maegan. In the back right was a Ken Griffey Jr. baseball card.

Noah scanned the space up and down, and then side to side. Near its opening and close to his left ear was a pile of papers he'd never seen before, wrapped neatly in a fraying cord of rope. It looked similarly to the story he'd put in a couple of months back. He pulled it out and shined the beam of dim orange light on the top sheet. The rain outside bounced off the roof more steadily. Noah sat himself down on the bathroom floor, propped his back up against the bricks below the opening, and began to read.

XVII

1/17/99

"Hey hold on!" I yell as I run into my house to get mittens. Right as I ran in I smelled delicious hot chocolate... no time I quickly thought dashing up my stairs. Out of my perriferels I see them laying on the radiator. Nice and hot. I put them on and jump down the stairs. I sprint outside and right on cue a snowball hits my face. I fall on the ground from the impact of the mightey sting. As I lay on the ground I only think of one name. Cilus. "C'mon dude" I say jokingly. "Had to" he whispered smiling at his feet. Our eyes finally meet and we break out in laughter. Cilus is the class

clown at school. Whether putting laxitives in our teachers coffee or glueing pencils to desks, Cilus somehow always finds a way to make someone laugh. "Hey let's hurry up!" Cilus said breaking the laughter. "Yeah dont want to be late!" I kindly reply. We headed off to the park to have a huge snowball fight with some friends from school. These were more Cilus's friends then mine. Even though Cilus and I are best friends, we have other groups of what my mom calls 'buds'. We stop walking and start to run really fast. Up ahead we see them. They wave to us. I wave back. "C'mon Cilus lets go" I say cheerfully. No response. "Cilus?" I say questionably this time. I look back to see him on the ground, in the fetal position clutching his arm. "Cilus!" I scream running towards him. The rest of the friends come. "Get an ambulance" I mumble.

4/29/01

My life stood stationary. I stared down at my untouched blueberry cobbler. I zoned out. All I heard was my body telling me that this couldn't be true. I pinched myself but I stayed in my nightmare. Tears rolled down my cheek onto the ground. I run outside into my yard, covered by 5 feet of snow and fall down.

5/13/01

I remember it like it was yesterday: I had woken up early enough to see the sun outside my bedroom window. The whole farm was foggy and the dogs were all still asleep. I could hear Mable snoring in the corner. I decided to leave her be for now. I could smell a bowl of oatmeal outside my door. Mom was up.

When I bit into it, the toast was as crisp as a fall day. I ate the whole thing in under 10 seconds. Everything was starting to get lighter now. I could hear a rooster crowing from the barn. Mom had left the kitchen and gone back to bed.

I knew that I didn't want to but I had to walk out to the barn. I took a gulp outside of the big front doors before I opened them up.

All the colts and fillies were getting up now but only a few were awake enough to look at me while I walked into the barn. When I got to the back I saw her. She was still so little in my eyes. I started to cry. I've known Poppy for so long now. My whole entire life in fact. I couldn't believe that this was the last day I would have with her.

When she noticed me, she came over and rubbed up against the side of me. I hugged her back. After rubbing out my tears onto her back I stood up and smiled. I held my hand down on my side and began to walk back to the big doors. Poppy followed.

We walked around the fields for hours that day. We ran up hills together, and we ran down valleys too. We layed down in the tall grass when she needed some breath. A few times she had some ticks on her that I had to take off. We went by the pens to see the chickens run around. She wasn't as scared of them as much this time. We kept walking, me talking to her and her listening to me. I didn't cry once and I couldn't stop smiling.

Back at the barn I dropped her off in her pen. I read her a story for her last time with me. I hugged her goodbye. I cried again this time, but I was smiling.

The next morning I woke up and knew Poppy was gone now. The smell of a bowl of oatmeal was coming from the kitchen. Mom was up so I got up and met her.

XVIII

NOAH sat with the stories for a bit. The tapping of the rain had grown to sound like a waterfall of pebbles plunking themselves down onto the Murphy's roof. Every word he'd read was narrating itself in his head using Maegan's voice—her tone, her pitch, her cadence. He was absolutely, unquestionably, undoubtedly, in love.

XIX

LOGIC would suggest that the ray of sunlight beaming down from the crown of the sky was what had made the cliff feel so warm, but Noah knew deep down that wasn't the reason why. The white wall felt as warm as it always had, rejecting cool breezes around its surface and glowing with a source Noah couldn't fathom.

The aforementioned trip that Noah and Maegan took to the cliff was on a Saturday; it was the seventh or eighth one they'd taken together. Each outing began the same way, with Maegan gaining a twenty-yard lead on Noah in the woods (though the last two trips Noah had made up some serious ground on her), followed by her waiting for him at the hole in the trees. Then, they'd walk their way on the riverbank for fifteen minutes, eventually being met with the boulders and cliffs that gradually became larger and taller. Once they'd reached the big white cliff, they took their shoes and socks off, stuffing the latter into the sole of the former. They spent some number of minutes (Noah found it difficult to keep track, as time always acted funny when he was with Maegan) with their arms sprawled against the face of the cliff, their chins squished up and on their sides. Maegan would come and tap Noah on the shoulder, and then the two would sit down on the sloped rock at the base of the cliff. They'd dip their toes in the cold rushing water and watch sticks be controlled by the current, talking all the while. Sometimes they'd map out perfect days to one another, and other times they'd debate which artificial fruit flavor is best; the prompts were endless. After their discussions, they'd sit next to each other with their feet up on the smooth rock and let the sun dry the river water off their ankles. Then, once the sun had dipped itself beyond the tallest of the trees, they'd pull their socks back on, slip into their shoes, and leave.

On that Saturday, Noah had been looking at the current of the river and thinking back to a camping trip he and his family had taken when Maegan nudged him with an elbow. He returned to the present in a sudden shake—the river had made his feet feel weightless and allowed him to zone out.

"I gotta get going now," she said.

"Get going?" he asked.

"Yes."

"Why?"

She paused to think.

"Dinner's soon," she said slowly.

"Dinner?"

"Dinner!"

"Alright," Noah mumbled. "You're not lying to me, right?"

"What?"

"You're not lyin-"

"Don't do that," she shot back, "and *no,* I'm not. My mom is having guests over tonight."

Other than a select few friends, Noah never heard of anyone else eating dinner over at Maegan's. He nodded, pushing against the sloped rock with the palms to lift his feet out the water.

"I'll save you some crisp. It's gonna be apple and plum," she said while scrunching her striped socks past her soaked heels. Noah couldn't help but smile at the prospect of eating dessert, and quickly all the ill-will he had towards her leaving early went out the window.

* * *

Ever since the night he'd seen his ghosts, Noah had been visiting the attic to see if they might come back. He mostly went after dinner, when the sun would set in a distant corner of the sky and the moon would rise in another. One night, the moon was waxing, only days away from reaching its fullness; it was big and bright, its craters clearly identifiable and the dark sliver of its body just barely contrasted against the navy-blue sky. Stars popped themselves up all over the place. June had begun, and with each day the weather became warmer, and with it the attic became stuffier. The hatch to enter was sticking from humidity, along with the corners of the window developing a layer of sweat on its sides.

Noah sat on an orange bucket he'd found hidden behind some dusty boxes at the far end of the room. He had his hands on his jaw, his elbows propped on his knees, and his feet turned in like a pigeon. It would appear to a fly on the wall that he was watching the sky change and the moon grow brighter and smaller, or maybe even studying the stars twinkle and piecing them together into made-up constellations. The moon, the stars, the woods, the field—they were all just unthreatening props that backdropped his thoughts. Although he'd declared that his sole intention of venturing to the attic was to look for the ghosts, he'd failed at doing so after his first few trips. His monitoring of the wood's edges was more infrequent than it'd once been, and eventually he stopped squinting at the shadows behind the blueberry bushes. He didn't even look at 'the rock'—a spot he'd once claimed to be his command post over the farm. As time passed, he became too occupied with worrying about growing up that he'd forgotten the spot existed. The mountain, the fort, the bed—all that 'the rock' had manifested into had disintegrated in the absence of Noah's imagination; it was now no more powerful than its name. So, instead of scanning the land, Noah let his mind drift off into his unfiltered thoughts. The attic seemed like the only spot in the world where he could reflect.

May had passed almost as fast as April had, and in swift time the school year would be over. Although he knew it to be impossible, all Noah wanted was for the world to pause. He wanted days to move like molasses, for the moon to stay in its same phase for a few days longer, for the warm weather to cease and for the hatch to open without sticking. He'd dwell on these kinds of thoughts often, and although he understood the ridiculousness of them, they were genuine and scary.

He didn't like middle school, and he especially didn't like eighth grade; everything was too supervised and unimportant for him. In a lot of ways, he wanted to be older. Warren kept mentioning how pretty the high school girls were. Change, in this regard, was good. However, every time he convinced himself to be gung-ho about the idea, he couldn't. He wanted to be older, but he knew, as strongly as he'd ever known anything, that he didn't want to grow up. He could feel it in his gut. He loved his house, his mother, his father; he loved being a big brother to Samuel and Sharon. Sometimes he even loved being a little one to Mack. He felt comfortable in his place, and he didn't want to leave it. In adulthood, he wouldn't be able to trot around on snow days, making big useless tracks back and forth in his yard. He wouldn't have the luxury of living rent free on his own platform in a big red farmhouse. The days of visiting the cliff with Maegan would end one day, too—he'd already begun moving his things out of their spot. The process now seemed somewhat symbolic.

The world Maegan had built inside the brick wall held all the tiny hidden corners in life, something she'd emulated so perfectly in her stories. Everything in Emmy's Hollow was something he loved—a collection of unique blocks that made him think more in depth about little things he wouldn't have found to appreciate at first. As Noah thought it, they were all now at risk of dying.

So as the shadows moved, and as the bushes rustled, Noah didn't notice. He just sat on the orange bucket, his feet turned in like a pigeon, his mind cautious towards the future. That night, the only spot he stared at was near the big rock, where he'd found the deer. Every time he looked in its direction, he was reminded of strawberry saltwater taffy and death. Once the sky had turned black, he made his way through the dark and flipped the hatch. Inside his room, he skimmed an article Mrs. Hannings had given him and added a few sentences to his final project on Pearl Harbor.

When he got into bed, the walls creaked and settled themselves into their place. Far off in the center of his house, he could hear the furnace rumble until it halted. He could hear his heartbeat, too—a lazy metronome that ticked as he turned to the last chapter of a book; it was an ending he'd read a dozen times now. Upon marking a corner of a page and placing its body next to his lamp, he stared outside one last time. He was truly too tired to think anymore; all he could do was look at the trees, now dense with bright green leaves, sadly swaying themselves to sleep.

XX

SHELLEY Avenue wound itself around the woods, glossed in a biblical rain that came down as fast as ever. As far as Noah could see, no cars were anywhere on it; behind the hills, around the bends—nothing. The sky had a velvety blackness to it, and the moon was new, looking as if it'd disappeared completely from the night's sky. No stars twinkled, and no airplanes crossed. If it weren't for his flashlight, Noah would be blind. He'd been running uphill for a while as fast as he possibly could; his ghosts were behind him, breathing loudly and getting closer. As he passed the road's summit, his knees had turned into soft noodles and his body went powerless. He slid down the blacktop, picking up speed, desperately clutching to the shaft of his flashlight as if it was a rope that kept him from flying into the ditches. Wind streamed onto his face; he could only see stripes of yellow and white lines zoom past his eyes. And then he was still, and so he stood up, looking ahead into the woods with his light illuminating a gap in the trees. His legs felt strong again. Without question and without thought, he ran in.

The forest was much drier than the road had been, though the density of the trees had made it impossible to move past them without scraping against one or two. Branches stuck out all over; they were shaped like hands, stretching out and snatching things that got lost in the darkness. Noah ran with haste, hopping over logs and overgrown roots, moving closer to a magnet with every step. Whispers from up ahead crept in, and although he couldn't make out words, he knew the voices wanted to stop him from seeing something. He was still being followed.

And so, he scrambled on, surely scratching his body against wood and rock as he passed. His light got swallowed by the thick darkness; for the forest regurgitated any brilliance that'd entered its walls.

He ran.

No shield could be made strong enough to prevent the transdermal presence of paranoia—an evil that soaked its way into his skin. The voices grew louder, hissing like demons and growling like wolves. He stopped running to turn and see if he'd lost his ghosts. It seemed like he had. Upon turning back around, he found light. Along the edge of the inky forest were thousands of holes lined up next to each other, stretching out forever to his left and right; there had to be millions of them. He ran again, sprinting straight ahead to the hole that was closest to him. Now almost through the one he'd chosen, instinct made him twist his head, allowing him to catch a glance before being swallowed up in the orange light. The holes he'd seen looked like a hall of mirrors that were stretching endlessly—millions of chambers, all leading to the unknown.

He'd reached the boulders of rocks that stepped themselves down to the riverbed. All but two whispers had subsided. He was sure where they were coming from but had trouble interpreting how such a thing was possible. He couldn't care less about his surroundings; for all he knew, there could be blank walls on either side of him, maybe even two above and beneath him. His focus was fully on the water ahead, which was black as a raven, and rushed itself over a muffled discussion between the unmistakable voices of a young boy and a woman.

Noah reached the bottom of the steps, his feet now not far from the edge of the river. He'd somehow become barefoot (where his socks and shoes had gone, he didn't know and didn't care). Upon reaching the shore, he dipped his toes gingerly in the water. To his surprise, it wasn't cold. In fact, it wasn't anything. The voices sounded concerned and depressed, but Noah couldn't catch any words. The boy sounded like Samuel, only slightly distorted. He waded out into the water as quietly as possible; his movement made sounds that made the voices harder to hear.

His flashlight was gone, and he saw white foam a few feet ahead of him. He stopped again, listening. The woman sounded like she was on the verge of spilling tears. Noah waded deeper towards their voices, worried who they were talking about, worried if they were in danger. He was horizontal now, kicking his legs as fast as he could to swim to his brother. When he dropped his head under water the voices disappeared. And then he was dragged down, like an invisible chain was wrapped around his neck. All hope of surfacing was lost—completely lost. He flailed his arms like a madman, straining his neck to get a look at the surface. Water pressure started compressing his head. A chill cloaked his body. His arms were outstretched, scratching and grabbing for anything. However, he kept swinging his hands and missing. He felt wrapped up, like a bug in its cocoon—all sweaty and trapped. Everything around him was dark, but also felt somewhat soft and forgiving.

And then he sprang up, gasping for air, looking out into the hallway beyond his opened bedroom door. His covers were all bunched around him, drenched in sweat. His pillows were on the floor beside him. He could feel his heart racing.

After regathering himself, his sheets were fully stripped. He changed his clothes, went to the bathroom, washed his face, and finally climbed back into his bed underneath a big blue blanket he'd found in the back of his closet. With his eyes forced shut, he flooded his mind with affirmations that what he'd dreamt had been illusory. Despite doing so, he still felt rattled. Outside, a light green haze was mixing itself with the jet-black starry sky. Dawn was only a couple of hours out. After several poor attempts, he'd fallen asleep, trying to forget about a familiar place far away.

XXI

BUT not too long after, he awoke (again). He looked outside his window; the moon was now high in the sky and much smaller than it'd been when he'd gone to sleep. The trees had stopped swaying. Unlike his dream, the sky was fully clear.

It was painfully quiet in his bedroom. No matter how high he raised his ears, Noah couldn't hear a thing. He didn't know how he knew, but he was certain that someone was near him; he felt it in his gut, only it was stronger than a normal rush of intuition—a sixth sense he possessed that alerted him when someone was behind him and staring. It sent a chill down his spine.

"I'm going."

The voice cut itself through the air so clearly that Noah knew it couldn't have been a hallucination on his part; it was the same voice that he'd heard in his dream, although this time he knew it wasn't Samuel's. This one sounded raspier and like it belonged to someone slightly older. The voice rang from underneath the foot of Noah's bed, and as curious as he was to check underneath it, his legs remained frozen like cold sticks.

A long silence fell; not even a cricket made a peep. While Noah listened, he could've sworn he'd gone deaf; for he could only hear a buzzing. Out in the hall, and to the left of his open door, a faint sound of wood creaking interrupted the flatlining atmosphere. By now, Noah had fully adjusted to the darkness around him, and was (just barely) able to see a long and skinny floorboard slowly rise from the ground and carefully be placed near the wall farthest from his room. Another floorboard was lifted and landed just as gingerly in the same spot. Noah's heart fluttered about like a hummingbird's wings. Whoever, or whatever, had moved the floorboards was now climbing their way out of the hole in the floor. If the air hadn't been so dead, there was a significant chance Noah would've gone back to sleep.

The figure crept their way into Noah's eyesight, scampering on all fours towards the floorboards they'd just taken out, resembling a shaggy dog. Noah still couldn't see their face, but he presumed it to be one of the ghosts he'd once spotted in the field. The figure fit the planks of wood back into their home as quietly and as cautiously as they'd extracted them. And then, they rose.

The outline of a boy was framed in the lines of Noah's

doorway for only a quarter of a second; it was all the time Noah needed to become more frightened than he'd ever been before. Whatever he was—a boy, a ghost, a spirit, The Devil—he was ingrained in Noah's mind, never to leave. His pointed nose; his long, tangled hair; his rib cage that poked out from the thin shirt he wore. All the scary stories and horror movies that Noah had been exposed to in his lifetime couldn't come close in matching this fear he felt. *Is he a ghost? What if Mack was right? What if we're being robbed? What if he's trying to kill someone?* The thought of the boy walking up the stairs of the middle house shocked Noah's body out of comatose.

His steps to the door were all on the tips of his toes. The possibility of the scene being a dream lingered in the back of his mind, and so he pinched the loose skin on his forearm until it stung too badly to continue. Once he reached the hallway, he stopped to listen. For a minute, he heard nothing but the buzzing; it was followed with slow, faint creaks—*tap. tap. tap.* The hallway, which had no windows, was much darker than his bedroom had been. He couldn't even see the staircase ahead. Now past the theory of still being asleep, Noah believed he'd gone mad.

Over time, his eyes had finally adjusted to the dark and allowed him to now see all the way to the top of the staircase. Out of fear, he'd unconsciously started pinching his arm again. *What now?* He was tempted to check what was under the floorboards, but then quickly ruled out the idea. While he contemplated his next step, he heard, or thought he heard (it was really too quiet to tell), a thud coming from the heart of the house. He moved upon instinct.

Each step down was met with a noisy squeak that echoed itself down the steps and into the hall below. *Why do mine sound so much louder?* He bounded two steps at a time, as if it would make things any quieter, with his right palm sliding with sweat down the old metal railing that lined the staircase. When he reached the bottom, he paused for a moment to listen. Again, all he heard was the buzzing of nothingness. And then he moved, striding his way across the smooth wooden floor of the main hallway until he'd swung a left and snuck into his parents' office. Although the moon was on the other side of the house, the window on the far end of the office gave enough light for Noah to scan. No one else was there. Overwhelmed, he grabbed the spinning chair tucked into his parents' desk and sat down. Parallel from where Noah sat was the staircase that led to the bedrooms. As scared as he was, he knew he had to go again. He gave himself three deep breaths to get fixed.

It took more like seven, but after he'd filled his lungs up to the gills, he got up from the seat and took his first stride towards the steps. As he made his way into the hallway, the boy cut him off. Noah could feel his heart drop into a chamber far below his stomach, accompanied with shock in every nerve of his body—a sensation as if lightning had struck him and set his arms and legs on fire. The interaction happened all too suddenly to make him scream, so the only noise he made was a shuttered breath. The boy was the same height as Samuel, just much, much skinnier. His nose was bent, his ears pointed, and his cheeks dirty. The boy had looked at Noah right in the eyes, and it was at that point in the night when he understood that what was happening wasn't a dream. Noah hadn't gone mad. For some inconceivable reason, there was a filthy boy hiding in the floorboards and running about his house in the middle of the night. After he'd locked eyes with Noah, the boy sprinted back up the same stairs he'd just came down. The aftershock in Noah's hands and feet made him buzz. He felt nauseous.

A minute of silence and shock passed before the stairs next to Noah sounded off with thuds. By the time his father had reached him, he'd already vomited a little in his mouth. They conversed in hushes—first Noah, explaining the intruder, and then his father, asking him to repeat himself; and so he did. As Noah spoke, he teared up, his throat growing taught and sore. The expression on his father's half-asleep face transformed from confused to disturbed. He paused, and then he nodded. Noah pointed up the stairs to his left. Without a word, he passed Noah and into his office. He reached behind the cabinet furthest from the door, pulled out a baseball bat, and made his way over to the staircase. Noah followed at his heel. Once his father had reached the top of the stairs he stopped on a dime, causing Noah to run straight into his back.

The hallway was, once again, deserted. Before Noah could whisper where the boy had gone, his father's hand was already held out to stop Noah from moving. He slipped into the open entrance of Noah's bedroom. He could hear his bed being flipped and his closet door open. Noah stood stuck in the dark, listening, for what felt like the hundredth time tonight. This time, however, he knew where the boy was. He was sure of it.

Noah's father emerged from the bedroom and made a beeline for the bathroom. Another attempt to get the attention of him was met with a stuck-out hand, telling his son to kindly: *'shut up and stay still'*. After a brief sweep of the bathroom, his father returned to the hallway. This time around, he walked until his head was directly under the latch to the attic. As he raised his hand to flip it down, Noah ran over and swung his hands around his father's arm.

It took what must have been a full minute for his father to wiggle free from his son's grip. For a second, Noah was preparing to be hit. At this point, though, he'd stopped caring; it didn't matter if he got punched. He pointed furiously at the ground beneath them until his father grabbed his arm and made him stop. Noah could see his confusion. However, he could also see faith starting to swim in his eyes. The buzzing from earlier had come back. Time stood still. Everything surrounding them was static.

"He's under the floor," Noah whispered, his voice so soft he could barely hear the words himself. "He took out the floorboards."

His father stood where he was, staring at Noah with the same gaze he'd held before. For a moment, Noah wondered whether he'd heard him. But then he nodded, and as Noah stepped back towards the wall, his father crouched to the ground and ran his hands against the floor.

XXII

EASTER Sunday and Christmas Eve were the two times of the year in which the Libby's went to church. With that being said, going on the third day of June was odd. Women wore sundresses, and almost all the Men had khaki shorts on. Members of the church had propped almost all the stained-glass windows along the sides of the chapel open a few inches to let June air waft in. Noah had no desire to be there, despite it seemingly being a great place for him to meditate on all that'd taken place. It didn't matter. He already had enough time to think. If anything, he now found it more laborious to replay the story again in his head. He hadn't slept in hours. If he had, it was only for a twenty-minute stretch of time. He scanned across the chapel at the artwork on the back wall, and then he closed his eyes. When the pastor asked all to kneel, he was one of the last to get down.

Upon kneeling, he peeped over at his family beside him. Sharon's sandals had flopped open when she'd pressed her knees to the rest, which revealed brown feet, all beat up from running up and down streets yesterday when she was catching lightning bugs. She'd been hunting with a boy whose name is Max—the youngest member of a family of devout Christians, and thus a loyal member of Woodrow's church. Max's family was sitting behind the Libby's by a few rows. Mack had to restrain Sharon each time her little sister would turn her head to make silly faces.

The profile of the boy Noah had seen was as clear as it'd been eight hours ago. His face hadn't left his mind for a second. The boy's mother, though—her face wouldn't leave his thoughts for the rest of his life. When he'd seen the boy, he could distinguish the superficial aspects of his face: the shape, the size, the dirtiness, the crookedness. When he'd seen the mother, he recognized emotions. Emptiness, guilt, anger, and sadness; it was all in her eyes, and those eyes cried, and cried, and cried. Noah couldn't understand how she hadn't run out of tears. He knew that they weren't caused by the pain from her leg (which was caked in dried blood and unusable, a result of it being broken horribly in an animal trap); the drops that she'd let go were heavier than anything that could be conceived from physical pain. She cried for her son.

Although Noah hadn't known that there was a storage unit beneath his hallway, his father had. Noah had overheard him tell the police that it used to be one of the spots where he'd kept hay and barbed wires (before both he and Noah's mother gave up on their dream of owning livestock). He hadn't checked on the spot in what he'd said had been a few years now. Besides the mentioning of the storage unit at the beginning of the report, Noah hadn't listened to almost any of what his father told the police. He'd zoned out to the max; it was all too surreal to comprehend. He wondered if Maegan had heard about any of it. He struggled to imagine ways in which he could explain everything to her. He kept asking himself what had happened and why in hopes of the off chance of enlightenment, fantasizing about discovering any kind of answer. It didn't have to be perfect by any means. All he knew was that he'd seen the son of a mother who cried heavy tears. Noah's own mother was tapping him on the shoulder. He was the only one still kneeling.

XXIII

SAMUEL'S bad mood began from the second the Libby's stepped out of the church doors and ended once he got some lunch into his belly. Noah's parents had decided that he and Sharon were both too young to figure out what had gone down; they'd stayed in their room for the entire night, door locked, and only learned from their mother that 'some people tried to take some things'. Thus, his complaints about sitting through a seemingly unwarranted June church session was understandable to the bunch who knew more. The island in the kitchen, a tall and sound wooden block shaped by Noah's father some years ago, had been cleared of papers on top of papers that detailed a hushed report. Its surface was now covered from corner to corner with crinkled parchment wrap, hot sauce packets, strands of lettuce, sesame seeds, bacon bits, empty tin soda cans, crumpled napkins, a fallen pickle, seeds from a tomato, and plastic cups that once held mayonnaise, now scraped clean and upside down.

In the minutes that preceded, all that could be heard was chewing, swallowing, and a burp or two. No one had eaten a proper meal in hours. For breakfast, they'd stashed granola bars into jacket pockets to eat on the ride over—a mix of apple cinnamon, chocolate chip, and peanut butter. When they'd been driving to the church, and when Noah had decided that it'd come time to eat his only morsel of food, the car had risen past a knoll to reveal the steeple. Fog rolled down the southern hills of the nature conservatory to his right and disappeared when they hit the forest line. A haze hung in the sky, not too thick to block out the light from the sun behind it, but also not too thin to harm any eyes that glanced up. The effect made Noah feel as if he were inside some gigantic snow globe. Between the knoll and the parking lot, he'd taken his time eating the bar, nibbling away at it in tiny chunks as if to make the breakfast any more filling.

Similarly to the sandwich he'd wolfed down, it would take a long time to digest all that'd gone on as of late. For now, he had to change; his button down was stained in Frank's Red Hot and his slacks had been covered with tiny crumbs of toasted bread. His toes hurt too; the socks that he'd worn were so thin that it felt as if he'd worn his penny loafers with two bare feet. He got up and put his plate next to the mess on the island, then walked over to the hallway.

"Where are you going?" Noah's mother asked; she'd spoken in synchronization with putting her own plate on the tabletop and rising from her seat.

"My room—I need to change."

"I could get things for you."

He stalled. After the incident, Noah had gone to his parents' room for the night. He hadn't been back up into his side of the house yet. Only hours earlier, his mother had made him repeat to her what had happened *exactly*—again, and again, and again. She'd rushed to her room during the breaks she had from the police, hugging him with each word he spoke, asking him if he was okay. She was being a mother.

"Okay."

* * *

Not an inch of clothes on Noah weren't gray. From his hoodie to his cotton t-shirt, from his sweatpants, rolled up several times at the cuff, to his wool socks below. After an afternoon nap, most of what he wore was drenched in sweat. Outside it was eighty, and inside it felt even hotter. Noah's parents' room had grown to be stuffed up, with windows sweating out big blots along their edges and the ceiling beginning to do the same. No one besides him was in the room. Judging from the shadows projected onto the rear wall, he knew it to be long past three P.M.

He convinced himself it was time to get out.

Upon reaching the last block that came down from his parents' bedroom, he quickly made a right and darted up the stairs to his platform. There it was—in between where the stairs flattened out and the entrance to his bedroom was a great hole in the ground, some five feet wide and eight feet long. Inside was a crammed mess. Canned food and wild fruit were in its corners. Hay was strewn about on the ground as some sort of makeshift bed. It resembled a coffin. The air was too stuffy to be safe, and the area too small to be cozy. Its far side had planks yanked out of it to escape. After several minutes of silent staring, he decided enough was enough, and it was time to shower. With each glance down at the hole, he thought of the mother—crying, and crying, and crying.

The shower he took was fast and cold. Noah's section of the house always grew to be the hottest come summertime. To him, the first week of June was the beginning of the season. Warm weather magically rolled itself in from the coast as soon as schoolwork eased up and melted away. Every year it would happen just like that.

It took several shoulder-leaning budges to break into his bureau; his room was even more stuffy than his parents had been. When he'd opened it, he threw on his bright purple *Libby's Locally Owned Blueberry Field* t-shirt and a yellow pair of shorts that bagged down to his kneecaps. No socks.

With one great scoop, he gathered all the gray cotton he could and threw it in a basket deep in his closet. As he shut the closet door, a faint shimmer from down below caught his eye. Tucked into the corner was an oyster shell; the white lining of the shell had caught a ray of sun that bounced off Noah's bedroom window. It sat atop a pile of coins, rocks, old paper, baseball cards—all that once had a home in Emmy's Hollow. Just as he'd figured that it was time to leave his parents' room, he knew he had to call Maegan.

* * *

He gave up trying to reach her after the fourth time had failed. He planned to walk down to her, just like he'd done so many times before, and meet her out on her clear porch, or maybe in the center of her garden. The heat gave him cabin fever. He was out of his house in a matter of minutes, only stopping in the kitchen, where he'd pulled the last remaining Sprite (which had 'Mack's' written in Sharpie on it) from the inside wall of the fridge. He snagged a hat at random from a box high up on a shelf in the mudroom and flew out the door, en route to the yellow lines ahead.

Now out on the hot pavement, the blistering sun crashed down onto the brim of his father's blue bucket, the floppiest hat in the entire world. More cars than normal came and went on

Shelley Avenue that afternoon, forcing Noah to walk in the ditch between the road and the trees for most of his trek. He came to a stop at the hairpin turn; it was the intersection that stood between Maegan's, Noah's, and the trail that led to the great white cliff. The sun blazed orange, the sky filled with baby blue, and a breeze, soft and low, rustled the surrounding trees. A feeling in his gut made his feet move to the branches behind him, made his head duck underneath them, made his legs walk through the mounds of dirt and over the mossy boulders. The woods were cool and more vibrant than they'd been in months. It was June.

He walked as he remembered: straight and far. It looked just like the dream he'd had the night before. He hadn't been to the cliff since he moved all his things out from Emmy's Hollow. In the past, he'd always followed her, trailing. That afternoon, though, he had no marker; for no sundress flapped in and out of eyesight. Because he'd gone so many times before now, it frustrated him when things slowly looked more and more unfamiliar. The farther he walked, the more he thought he could hear the rush of water, absentminded to the leaves that shook in the wind above him. He climbed over rocks and stepped from exposed root to exposed root. The scene's beauty distracted him; the sun was now at an angle that made the woods look like Eden. Its shine streamed through thousands of thin, green-colored films, illuminating the entire floor in its shadow. Not before long, Noah hit a wall of thorn bushes. A 720 degree turn confirmed that he'd gotten lost.

With an air of defeat, he pulled the Sprite can out of his baggy yellow shorts. Mack's writing had smudged. The green can matched the color palette of the atmosphere perfectly; it was as if it'd been made specifically for him to have right then and there. It tasted cooler than cool—the paragon of refreshing. In three big sips and in four big burps, it was gone. He put it down on the dirt and crushed it underneath his flip-flop, tucking the flattened aluminum into his shorts. Then, he turned around to walk back in the general direction of where he'd come from. It all looked the same to him. Thousands of trees lined each direction he looked. Their trunks rose and fell over identical slopes. The sun helped; he followed the shadows in hopes of them spitting him out somewhere on Shelley Avenue.

Minutes of walking passed by. He eventually got nauseous, and his heartbeat sped up a couple of beats. The array of greens and browns that the forest displayed made Noah dizzy; it was as if he was stuck in some sort of time loop that was impossible to escape and never ending. All the bark felt the same, too: hard, scratchy, sappy, cold.

And then, in an instant, he recognized something in the scene that was *not* the same. Some fifty yards away was a color not brown or green, but blue—bright blue. The color took shape as a whale, screen printed on the front of a shirt worn by a girl with brown hair, freckles, and was the same height as Noah himself. The same feeling that he had when he'd finished reading Maegan's stories rose inside of him again. He sprinted in her direction.

She was so shocked to hear footsteps running her way that her surprise almost knocked Noah down to the ground. She remarked at how unsettling it was. He apologized, and she accepted. He was angry with himself for not knowing she'd been zoning out. Noah found an indescribable beauty in seeing her walk alone in the forest. She, like him, had ventured to the wall to seek refuge. Maybe she even went to find him, he thought. *Did she know?*

"Do you know?" he asked.

"About what?" she returned.

"So, you don't know."

She shook her head. Noah couldn't believe this to be true. *Did Sam and Warren know? Did anyone?* Despite saying she hadn't heard the news, Noah's stomach got queasy the way it always did when someone lied to him. She frowned slightly, but still frowned, and her eyes were glazed over too. After a deep breath, he started from the top. He told her about the attic, about the orange bucket, the circle window, the view, and the ghosts that he'd seen. He described their milky skin, their sharp bones. He told her about the scream that he'd heard. And then, he told her about the night before, something that in his head felt much longer ago than only a matter of hours. He told her about the noises that made him sit up in bed. He told her about the floorboards, the quietness, the darkness. He told her about his father coming, the baseball bat, the chase, the discovery. The police. The crying. The hugging. The interrogations. The dread. The re-explaining. The fatigue. The alertness. The sadness. He told her all.

And she listened to it all, letting him explain every bit. No interruptions. A hand on the arm, but no interruptions. She let him finish and then hugged him tighter than ever—a hug that spoke a million words. She didn't have to say a thing.

And at first, she didn't. At first, she cried, all the while holding on to Noah, her hands locked together around his back. He could feel his throat become tight. After catching a breath, she expressed her greatest sympathies and told him how horrible the story was, how awful she felt for him. She could only get a few words out at a time.

After a few minutes, she let go and looked him right in the eyes. Her eyelids were scarlet and had been puffed up an inordinate amount. Her hair was all messy. Her cheeks were stained with lines of tears that led down to her neck. She reached down and grabbed his hand, each of their fingers slipping into the other's notches. They walked back.

A significant moment of silence ended in her breaking it. She spoke again, this time about something different from crying mothers and loose floorboards. She told him about a place far, far away, like she was reading the opening lines of a folktale that Noah had read in the past and forgotten. The place was a pretty home. She described windows, great enormous windows, scattered across walls that were taller than Noah's home. A porch, made from strong brown wood, wrapped itself around the entire house, only interrupted by an outdoor shower and wide front steps. At the bottom of the steps was a walkway made of tiny stones, slithering themselves in a pathway that cut through bunches of flowers and fruit bushes. The backyard was huge, too. A chicken coop was set up not too far away from the shower. She'd painted a grand image—a great distraction to a terrifying story.

At least, it was until it wasn't. It was until she cried, and it was until the moment that Noah felt a pit in his stomach, like he'd swallowed lead. It wasn't a folktale. Maegan had described her home, her *new* home. Far, far away turned out to be a town near Keene, New Hampshire, and so he cried as well.

XXIV

DUSK came fast for a June night, or so it felt for Noah. He and Maegan had sat down on a massive boulder they'd found in the same neck of the woods where they ran into each other earlier. Hours had passed, and many things were said between the two. Under pressure to do so from Noah, Maegan had taken a deep breath and explained her situation first. She'd answered all his why's, when's, what's, and how's as best she could. She'd known for two weeks now, and she'd be driving to New Hampshire tomorrow to start the whole ugly and drawn-out process of transferal. She had to pause several times to comfort Noah and his tears. He wasn't ashamed of crying at all. He didn't care— now wasn't the time to feel embarrassed. For Noah, a middle school aged boy whose only worries in the world revolved around change and girls, the news rocked him to the core. It seemed like his childhood was on its deathbed, yet no bone in his body felt that he was being melodramatic.

It was when the mosquitoes bit at his ankles that Noah asked if she'd like to walk back in the road's direction, and so they did, hand in hand, one leading the other. The kaleidoscope of greens and yellows had died when the sun dipped under the hills on the far side of the river. No longer illuminated in evergreens and honeycomb, the forest settled under a cloak of brown. The air was still warm, and a breeze was still at play. As the two got closer to the edge of the forest, they'd gradually gotten a better view of the wildly dazzling display of orange dashes of light, all rapid and temporary in their performances. They flew from right to left and from left to right at chest level, just barely providing a gleam on the trees that lined the partition. Noah imagined the vignette they created on the corners of the road ahead, like a frame of a painting that kept changing outside of the front windshield.

Getting back on the road (or to the intersection, as Noah imagined it) at twilight felt symbolic. The day was closing, and they now had to leave each other to go back home. They hugged for a long time. When Noah let go, he opened his eyes; everything was so grainy, and the colors in the sky were soft and sad. It looked like a somber movie he'd seen before but forgotten the plot of. He wanted to say that he loved her. However, he was afraid, and so the words stuck in his throat forever. She turned right, and he turned left. She'd told him earlier that she'd see him tomorrow before getting on the road. Noah felt like they'd said it all and more. Now it was time to go back home and fall asleep. He was ready for the day to be over, and so he walked homebound, moving off the pavement and into the roadside ditch at the sight of faded yellow brighten behind the hilltops on Shelley Avenue.

* * *

Noah's parents were worried sick. According to them both, he'd been gone for close to six hours now. He hadn't left a note, he hadn't told a soul where he was going, he hadn't told a soul *that* he was going. All his siblings were upstairs; Noah imagined them with their ears cupped on their doors, listening to the scene in the living room unfold. As both his mother and father kept talking, their voices grew until they yelled at him. He could hear their voices, but he didn't listen to what they were saying. He didn't care. All he could do was think about Maegan and the mother underneath the floorboards. Both thoughts were dreadful in such a way that he couldn't fathom, linked in a profound way that he couldn't explain.

He was hungry, too; the sandwich and granola bar had worn off, and he could feel the beginnings of tremors in his stomach. Although it wasn't the appropriate time to ask to ask for dinner, he didn't care. He'd lost all hope on that day.

"Can I get dinner please?"

He'd interjected at a moment when his mother had stopped ranting to regather herself. They both looked up at their son, neither able to give an immediate response to his question.

"I'm hungry, and I haven't—"

"Yes," interrupted his mother. And with that, Noah didn't feel she was mad at him anymore. Her eyes were tired. She looked sad.

"There's pizza in the fridge—on the bottom shelf," said his father.

* * *

After he ate the final three slices and threw out their greasy cardboard container, Noah decided it was time for the worst day of his life to come to a close. In passing the living room, Noah saw that Maddy was fast asleep on the rug, grateful that the shouting had subsided and that the room had cleared. He felt both exhausted and restless going up to his parents' room— another moment of contradiction in a backward day. His legs felt like jelly, just about to give way and make him fall, but also shook with anxiety and made him skip a stair with each step. He understood why he was to stay in his parents' room, and he knew that tonight wasn't the night to argue back, yet he wanted to be in his messy closet more than anything, rummaging through the corner, reliving the memories that he'd shared with Maegan. He'd been awake for close to a full day now, and if it wasn't for the emotional fatigue that weighed on his body, there would be no chance he'd be able to sleep for hours. He settled in the middle of his parents' bed, his mind racing with all sorts of thoughts, taking their form in anonymous voices. They rushed at him with such speed that he couldn't understand what they said. All he could hear was their tone and pitch. His muscles had fallen asleep—just his mind was up, tiptoeing at the precipice of rest. An array of red dots shifted and rippled about beneath his closed eyelids, then blue dots, then green. And then he was asleep, not to wake for many hours upon the morning he dreaded.

XXV

AS her Volkswagen shifted gears and climbed the hill, Noah had no choice but to turn his head away. The blue sky, the red car, the bungee cords strapped from handle to handle; it was the saddest and sharpest and most significant image he'd seen in a while—maybe ever.

The chances are great that if he'd turned his head back around, he could've seen the bumper one last time, yet he couldn't let that happen. He was convinced that what he'd seen was written to be the finale. Any more would spoil it.

He stared at his shirt and analyzed tufts of cotton pull away from the stripes. He felt his throat grow tight. He saw some drops fall past his body. And when he finally turned around, she was gone.

XXVI

THE lemonade Noah drank was so tart that after two sips he reluctantly put it down for good. He was given it as a gift from Sam and Warren; they'd visited him during the window of time between Maegan's departure and nightfall. On the earlier side of that window, they'd rang the doorbell outside the mud room; it was the first time either had done so—Sam had always just gone right in (and, when doing so, almost always made a beeline right for the fridge to see what was inside). Warren would always follow. Mack had answered the bell, who then told Sharon to tell Noah that there were guests asking to see him, who then came to his room a-knocking (after Maegan had driven off, Noah's mother had allowed him to return to his wing permanently). It took him a few minutes for him to wipe his eyes.

The two boys were sitting together on the sinking coach in

the kitchen by the time Noah had made his way in. They were playing chopsticks with one another to keep busy. Warren spotted Noah first and tapped Sam on the shoulder.

"Hey, No'," began Sam. No matter how bashful he became, he still came across to Noah as the goofiest person in the whole world. "What's up?"

"Nothing, really."

Both of Noah's friends smiled a sad smile. It was once he had fully come into the kitchen and sat himself down on a stool that Warren picked up the plastic bag he had at his feet and handed it over to Noah. A Charleston Chew the size of a ruler topped a bottomless bag of chips and candies—a neon sea of cellophane. Warren visibly shifted in his seat.

"The Sir gave us the Brisk for free —" he said, his finger pointed to the twenty-eight-ounce bottle, "— he said he'd heard about the squatters. He says that he's sorry about that."

Noah didn't respond simply because he didn't know how to.

"And we're sorry too," Sam interjected.

Both Warren and Sam stayed for a bit after to talk about the happenings around school. After a slow progression, Noah was transported back to being a lively boy, eating junk food and talking with great importance about unimportant things alongside his two best friends. During their dishing, Noah brought up Maegan in an innocent sort of context to test if the others had heard the news yet; it was assumed they hadn't. Noah was much too tired to even begin explaining the situation. Instead, he let the news of Drew Carlin's new ('ugly') boyfriend die out.

It was after Warren had finished his rant that Noah announced his plans to take an afternoon nap. Sam and Warren were going off to a big hill on Morris Avenue (a ways away) with plans of taking turns lying belly down on a skateboard and zooming down its face. Warren berated Noah with invitations, but he insisted he must go to his room and recharge. While the visit was nice, Noah's social battery ran low fast, and he felt as if the only way to keep from becoming anxious was to be alone. The boys left. Noah went upstairs.

In his room, he continued to sift through the pile of things that'd once lived in the hole of Maegan's brick and polka-dotted bathroom wall. Before Sharon had come to get him, he'd looked at each item and remembered all the stories that accompanied them. Prior to their eviction, they made up a world beyond the one Noah envisioned himself living in. Everything put into Emmy's Hollow was a stitching of its soul—a story only special for two, but the *most* special for two. Now, the antiques, the rarities, the stories, the sketches, the rocks, whatever Noah had brought, and all the rest—they felt like they'd lost their lives. Still, he dug more than he could help. He'd periodically move to his bed or listen to his radio, but without fail he always went back; it was too windy for him to go out, anyway. The call for dinner served as an intermission to it all.

* * *

With plates cleared and bellies full, the Libby's split up after dinner. Every member of the family had migrated into a different corner of the house. Each flipped on a light and in turn created their own scenes, backdropped by yellow, framed in glass panels for the occasional traveling car or truck to digest; for no shades were drawn. Their silhouettes told stories—a girl brushed her hair away from a book whose pages were flipping over faster than most, a woman typed finances reports while facing the road below her, a little boy sprinted from scene to scene in smiling fashion, a man with his back to the yard ran his hand through his hair, a little girl recited her lines to the man for her part in the end of the school year play, and another boy, who was a little older than the one running around, sat all alone in the front, privately watching another performance on the fence across from his own.

Four people sat in a circle between the far field and Shelley Avenue. Noah had trouble discerning any of their facial features; the moon was strong, but it only revealed so much. They looked to be around Mack's age, but they were people he'd never seen before—two girls and two boys. The shorter boy and the shorter girl both sat up on the fence. The other two were sitting down and kept pointing up at their friends above, signaling random movements to one another. They both looked happy. He was under the assumption that the two sitting on the fence were happy, too. They passed around a cigarette every one or two minutes, skipping the taller boy on the ground each time a full trip was made around the circle. It looked warm out, even with a breeze that made its way over the hills, rippling the backs of the shirts of the boy and the girl on the fence. They made him think of Sharon and Samuel for a reason he didn't know at the time, or, more accurately, a reason he didn't know at the time because he wished to not dig into its intricacies. He understood the parallel his mind had attributed; it was easier for him to dismiss thoughts like those before they'd feed on his fears and transform into reality.

Later, when he was back in his bedroom, he ran his fingers over the top of an arrowhead he'd found weeks ago. He looked at it under his lamp as if he was a surgeon. Outside, the wind was whipping. The moon had already reached high in the sky, too. Noah noticed neither. On that night, the moon was as full as it could be; it was a mild pink—a strawberry moon.

He folded the arrowhead in the palm of his left hand, flipping it over on itself as he stared at the floor, unfocused on reality. Noah hadn't even noticed the last notes from Frederick's adaption of Liszt's *Die Forelle* hang out in the June air. If Noah *had* heard them, he would've thought the same thing as always: *how sad and lonely.* In his mind, no one ever had heard, and no one had ever appreciated, and no one had ever cared. Hours passed, and it wasn't until the dead of the night when he settled over the covers on his bed. He thought about the mother he'd seen and wondered if she was with her little boy. He thought of her face, sad and skinny. He also thought of Maegan. He thought of her garden. He thought of her face too, all grained out on the road. A train whistle went off somewhere in the countryside. He looked at his walls—one, by one, by one, by one. He needed to leave now.

So, he sat up and left.

FINAL CHAPTER

XXVII

BAREFOOTED and anxious was Noah that night. After making the ultimate decision to leave, he tip-toed across his bedroom floor, now stained in pink moonbeams and skinny shadows from the shaking leaves of the great elm tree. All was quiet, as no more voices sounded underneath his feet. The hall was darker than his room, but his eyes had adjusted well enough to make out everything. The staircase looked further away than normal, and it wasn't until he'd seen it that he recalled the creaking boards, which, if stepped upon, would pop and grind from the June humidity. A trip downstairs would be impossible. He stood there, in the middle of the hallway, with his hands in his short pockets and his eyes glued to where the alley ended— thinking, thinking, thinking.

He mapped out the entire layout of his home in his head, as

if he was a Western European art thief planning which Monet he was going to steal. If, somehow, he thought, he could get down to the first floor unnoticed, he'd still have to make it past the middle staircase of the home. And then, if his parents, who always kept their door open, still hadn't heard him, he'd have to make it through the kitchen, down the short step to the mudroom, and open both a wooden and a screen door of which Noah knew one was bound to make a great deal of noise. This was all going to happen two nights after a group of squatters were caught in the house. Calling the chances of escaping slim to none would be a poor over-exaggeration.

The pink dashes of light that filled Noah's room with dull warmth had crept their way out onto the floor of the hallway, just barely stretching to the far wall. He took his eyes off the staircase and moved them down to look at the light; it was just a sliver, a stripe of moonlight, surrounded by an entire platform of inky shadows. But out of all the dark spots in the hallway, it illuminated a spot that gave it purpose, and consequently provided a solution to Noah's ongoing dilemma. The streak ran right across the chipped endings of the same floorboards that'd been taken out two days prior.

The idea that charged through Noah seemed so wildly adventurous and unbelievable that it shot a rush of blood into his head. Everything in his mind was all twisted now. The voices he'd heard rush past him had returned, and in great fashion, too. He was lightheaded, and as he reached down to lift the board closest to his feet, his heart beat out of his chest. One plank up. Two up. Three up. Four.

His hallway (again) had a hole in its center filled with pitch black darkness. The sliver of light had spilled down into the hole, as if it was water in a baggy that'd been poked open at its bottom. The line of lonely light revealed the base he'd seen before. For minutes he stared and contemplated his next move. The pitch black turned a shade lighter, but just barely. The spot had been swept clean.

Still barefooted (and even more anxious now), Noah slowly lowered himself down. The landing was so soft that he could only just hear his feet touch the ground. He got down on his hands and knees, lowering his head beneath the floor of the hallway and crawling his way to the corner exit. Everything around him was cloaked in darkness, and, even with the slight adjustment his eyes had made, he could only barely tell a difference between his surroundings when his eyes were open versus when they were closed. In a mad attempt to contextualize where he was in relation to the exit, he flung out his arms at the wall, jamming his middle finger into a board of wood. It hurt badly, but he only winced.

After letting himself recover, he read the walls as if they were brail. He felt the corner that once had a hole in its side; it was a wooden wall, nailed down like all the rest that surrounded him.

In an act of anger and claustrophobia, he jammed his good hand into the corner. It gave way, though just a bit. He tried again, this time using the good hard bones at the bottom of his palm. It gave way a bit more. Again, again, and again, he slammed his hand, stopping for minutes in between so as to not wake anyone up. The wood broke on the eleventh try and fell onto the mess below. In his hindsight, Noah should've known that his father would board up the wall. Too late; it was broken. He crawled through the hole and popped out onto a skinny platform five feet below him.

His tiptoes down the barn steps were met with Percy's coming up. Both stopped, struck that they've seen one another at such an odd time and in such an odd spot. Percy was stiller than still, his eyes bright blue and vacant. As if they'd counted down to an agreed time, both cat and boy made their moves to pass each other in the same fraction of a second—one going up, and one going down.

After hopping down the last step, Noah quickly unfastened the rope that locked the two big front barn doors together. He pushed his way out, closed the doors gingerly, and turned towards the fields, now all scattered with baby bushes. His whole body shook, not from the wind and cold, but from the fear of what he was doing.

He ran.

He didn't know where he was running to, but that, to him,

didn't matter. He went faster than he'd ever before, flying through the vertical lanes of his family's field, blueberry bushes on each side of him acting as lanes like those on a track. The cold air crashed against his legs and chest in such a powerful way that it eventually numbed his skin. He could feel that he was running, surely, but the numbness of his body made his mind feel fully disconnected from the legs that took him where he was going. He never had a runner's high quite like that one.

At the end of the field, he only sped up. Mindful of where he'd set the traps months ago, Noah ran through a spot he knew to be safe. He then crossed the line between field and wood—illuminated and entrenched, clear and crowded. The anonymous voices screamed.

The trees in the forest shook from the wind; leaves fluttered about, and massive trunks swayed. Meanwhile, he moved like never before, hopping from root to root with no trouble at all, dashing between evergreens growing denser and denser with each advance. He could see the moon through the tops now, pink and huge; its craters formed the face of a man he'd seen before. The wind was louder than ever—swishing, swishing, swishing. He thought he heard an owl, and then he thought he hadn't. *What do owls sound like again?*

The more he ran, the more frightened and insane he grew. Herds of dead deer were all around him. The whole thing was contradictory—running farther into an environment he was terrified of, yet his legs couldn't turn back. He wasn't running away from the woods, but instead escaping a storm of changes that were fast approaching, snipping at his ankles with balls of hail and ropes of rain to trip him up. He ran to catch up with whatever was left in an era of his life—a frame of time he hallucinated as something that follows a script and dies in an inevitable death.

He cried.

The tears blinded him, but it didn't matter. It's not like he'd looked where he was going, anyway. His legs kept chugging. He hadn't tripped, or hit a tree, or stumbled the slightest. Everything happened with such ease. He thought that the wind howled stronger than it'd just a moment ago. He thought he heard another owl. His feet hurt—badly, too. His thighs were sore. His chest was tight, and his stomach had cold cramps stitched onto its sides. He kept crying. All the surrounding darkness suffocated him—a presence so strong and sinister that it felt like he breathed it in each time he gulped for air. The mother and her son weren't the only ones who watched; the spirit was still out in the woods, alive and awake, watching like The Devil—an illusion Noah had manifested to exist as a palpable embodiment of evil.

And then, as if he'd been teleported in the time it would take someone to snap their fingers together, he was floating. He never had such a feeling of complete weightlessness; even in water, he felt the pull of gravity against his body. The atmosphere was deathly quiet as he fell; for his ears had blocked out all sounds. He didn't scream, or say anything, rather. He didn't have time to be fearful of his position, as it was much too unexpected and unbelievable. As he spun, all he could see was the pink moon in his peripherals, falling in and out of sight as his body turned over on itself, and all he could think was: *what happens next?* He imagined himself tumbling into a great bowl of sand and somersaulting down until it flattened out at the bottom, where he'd lie on his belly and be fine. An instant after envisioning the dunes, his brain switched to consider a darker possibility. *Death?*

Noah's journey through space and time ended with the thunderous sound of his bones bouncing off the hard Earth. His back had hit the surface before his body bounced up and fell onto its side. His right cheek, now bloodied and torn open, faced the moon. Two barefoot feet pointed at the cliff behind him. It stood tall, straight, and was white as milk. The sound the impact had made was loud enough to travel from one camp to the next. However, no person heard anything of the sort. Only the evergreens had, which were swaying and fluttering, and the wide-eyed owls, and the Kennebec—rushing and swirling. It all ended there—thirty days past fourteen, and not a day more.

As the moon rose and shrank, the base of the cliff had grown feet of burgundy. The sloped rock was slick. A slow slide down its face and into the river began. Noah slipped in slowly, his face submerged first and his feet the last. Blood trickled its way into the river and was instantaneously diluted in the current. The moon still rose, the water still rushed, the trees still shook. Even sometime later, an owl gave a hoot.

In the coming hours, his mother would wake up, and like all the mornings that'd come before, she'd be the first one downstairs. With a flick and a whoosh, she'd start the stovetop and put her oats in with some water. Another pot would heat in the back until it whistled. A few minutes later, she'd bring her oatmeal (now mixed up with one scoop of peanut butter, two of Greek yogurt, a few dashes of cinnamon, blueberries, and gobs of honey) along with her cup of coffee into the living room. She used the same bowl, wide and gray and shallow, and the same cup, skinny and tan and tall. She'd be in the same spot, wrapped up on the couch in the blanket that she folded each night just to unravel again hours later.

ABOUT THE AUTHOR

Robby Sheils is a 20-year-old author born and raised in Portland, Maine. *Shelley Avenue* is his first novel. In 2019, he graduated from Portland High School. He is currently a student at Bates College and a member of the graduating class of 2023. Robby began writing *Shelley Avenue* in Rangeley, Maine during his winter break in January 2020.

CPSIA information can be obtained
at www.ICGtesting.com
Printed in the USA
FSHW012252291221
87284FS